All the Deadly Secrets

Carol Schaal

This is a work of fiction. Names, characters, places, and incidents are either drawn from the author's imagination or used fictitiously. Any resemblance to actual events or persons, living or dead, is entirely coincidental.

Cover design by Kerry Prugh

In memory of my mom, Gert, who loved mysteries and always asked, "What shall I read next?"

And to Jim, my ever-fixed mark.

All the Deadly Secrets

1

White holiday lights still glittered like shards of ice along Alleton's main street, and the Lake Michigan coastal village's many cute shops looked pinched. It was as if the buildings were clenching their steel joints together, trying to keep out the evening's piercing cold. I could relate.

As I often did, I wondered what Drew would have made of my new place, of the quaint Michigan town I'd fled to from Florida after his death made my life a hellish disaster. But I forced myself to dismiss those thoughts. I did not want to go to the party looking sad and lonely, although that is precisely what I am.

The Waves End sign said the art gallery was closed, but the side door was unlocked for the shop owners attending the January Doldrums gatherings, a Sunday night event. In the gallery's foyer I gazed at the tall metal sculpture of a young person of indeterminate gender, who was reaching for something unseen with fingernails of decorated upholstery nails. "Chill," I told the statue, whose steely resolve I always found disturbing. Then I headed up the stairs to the apartment where the gallery's owners, Frank Severino and Justin Noah lived. The smell of fresh-baked cookies welcomed me as I opened the door, beating out Frank's greeting by a good two seconds.

"Lauren! The angel of mercy arrives! Are you dumping

the Dragon Lady for us?" Frank, standing tall by the kitchen's large stainless-steel stove, wore an apron announcing, "Hot Stuff Coming Through." He twirled the spatula he held and bowed grandly.

"I've only come to grab some food for her. Maybe that will dampen her fearsome flames," I said. "That broken arm is making life hard for her."

Frank shook his head, shaved bald to hide the sign of a disappearing hairline, a look of aging the 40-something despised. "Too bad it wasn't a broken nose. Bernice sticks that in everybody's affairs."

He grabbed a paper plate and began to put together a serving of appetizers and cookies. "Was this part of the deal? She sold you the shop in exchange for cold hard cash and a weekly homage? If so, you got cheated. She should pay you for hazardous duty."

"Nah, I promised Sarah, who desperately needed a vacation. She agreed to continue working for me at the shop if I'd look in on her mother while she's gone."

"Some promises are stupid. And if I were you, I'd look for a knife in Sarah's hand. She must be furious that her mom sold the shop to you." Frank shrugged, then shooed me toward the apartment's main living area. "Poke your sweet self in there and tell everyone hello," he ordered. "Otherwise they'll think you're ignoring them. Of course, I'd ignore 'em too if they weren't my guests."

"Oh, now, what would you do for an audience?" I asked, then scurried away before Frank could swipe at me with the spatula.

When I turned the corner into the arched passageway, I heard the distinct growl of Dennis Tomlinson's voice. I had been in Alleton for only 10 weeks but already I knew that Dennis was constantly giving his wife, Tami, a hard time about, well, just about everything.

"Yeah, so getting the new inventory software right before Christmas was stupid. Yeah, it took too long to set up. But you just wait and see. It'll save us time soon."

Tami's response was soft, but standing around the corner, hidden from view, I could picture her chubby face red with embarrassment. "Den, it's okay. We can straighten it out. We had a good season, why don't we celebrate that?"

The Tomlinsons owned a toy and game store, one of the most charming shops in southwest Michigan's popular lakeside art colony. The Wooden Block had passed to Dennis following his parents' death in a car accident a decade ago, but everyone knew Tami did most of the work, and everyone felt sorry for her.

I peeked around the side of the open entry and saw eight or nine people standing near the apartment's custom half-circle bar, looking uncomfortable. I heard the low undertone of Justin, co-owner of the gallery, whose quiet demeanor offered a nice contrast to Frank's outsized personality, trying to guide the conversation to a lighter subject. I stepped back from the corner and returned to the kitchen.

"Bernice will be better company tonight," I told Frank. "I'm staying out of there. The Tomlinsons are at it again."

"Ah, yes, the joys of marriage," Frank said, then held out the foil-wrapped package. "Maybe this will help sweeten Bernice's disposition."

"Someone needs to sweeten Dennis's," I said as I took the plate. "And you are a sweetheart for putting this together. I owe you one. And don't tell anyone I was here. They'll wonder why I didn't say hello."

* * *

A couple miles from Bernice and her daughter Sarah's house, sleet was spitting at my SUV's windshield. I clutched the steering wheel, my shoulders tight. Florida born and raised, I was still tense about winter driving. When I finally pulled into the long driveway leading to the ramshackle farmhouse, I let out the breath I didn't realize I was holding. The aroma of Frank's chicken satay and artichoke dip had dissipated, leaving only a chill in the car's cabin.

Strange, just a dim light showed from the kitchen. I grabbed the foil package of goodies, walked to the side door, and knocked. After waiting a couple minutes, I fished out the key Sarah had given me.

I stepped into the kitchen, lit by the oven hood's dome light, and automatically glanced down, expecting to be greeted by Eliot, the big tabby. On my previous visits, he had welcomed me at the door, but now he was nowhere to be seen. Neither was Bernice. I plunked the food package down next to a plate of thumbprint cookies and a tea cup sitting on a nearby counter and called out. "Bernice? Mrs. Mullins? It's Lauren Andrews. Hello?" No response.

I walked across the oak flooring of the kitchen and peeked into a utility room that held a washer and dryer. A furnace hulked in the corner. No one there. I turned to the living room, then checked the nearby bathroom and downstairs bedroom. Empty. The door that opened on the stairway leading up to Sarah's household quarters was locked, but when I pressed my ear against the wood surface, I heard no movement above. The house felt empty and was starting to creep me out. Bernice knew I was coming, and the woman who let me know at our first meeting that she would not put up with latecomers, and thank goodness I hadn't been late, was not one to miss an appointment.

Taking deep breaths, trying to control my panic, I did another circuit of the downstairs. I threw back the bathtub's shower curtain, opened the bedroom's closet door, peered under the bed. The only sign of Eliot was a worn chew toy on the floor, and the only sign of Bernice was her oversized black vinyl purse on top of a tall dresser.

The abandoned purse was not a good sign. Bernice carried it everywhere. But maybe, I thought, maybe Bernice had to make a quick run to the store or maybe a friend had picked her up and maybe Bernice had only needed her small coin purse. Only one way to find out. I hesitated, then decided it was okay to snoop given the circumstances. I opened the purse, first glancing warily around as if Bernice might suddenly appear to give me hell for violating her privacy, and saw a Kleenex package, lip balm, comb, an empty prescription bottle, two pens, a business card, a small notebook. And the coin purse.

I pulled my jacket close, even though the house was warm, and returned to the kitchen. One other door there caught my eye. Oh no, the basement. Visions from horror movies danced in my head — don't go in the basement! — so I flipped a light switch at the top of the stairs and went down only the first two steps. From there, I could see it was just a small room with a chest-high shelf running around the walls, stocked with canned goods. It had a dirt floor and odd, musty smell, but otherwise the dim, dusty space was empty.

I walked back to the kitchen and hesitated at the door leading outside. The house had no nearby neighbors, and the isolation and winter's early darkness were getting to me. Sarah had told me cell phone service was nonexistent in the area, which meant I couldn't call for help while in the backyard if a man or beast attacked me. "Stop imagining monsters," I told myself. The pep talk wasn't much help. It wasn't monsters I feared, but a real live person, hiding in the dark, knife or gun in hand.

Inhaling deeply, I finally was hit by the one possibility that galvanized me into action. Bernice might need me. Not giving myself any more time to think, I turned on my phone's flashlight app and headed outside. I walked quickly on hard-frozen mud to the garage and pulled on the small entry door. The sight of Bernice's rusty old Chevy wagon, sitting there silent and unhelpful, almost made me cry. "Okay," I whispered to myself, "so she didn't take the car. That doesn't mean anything." I stepped into the garage, looked inside the car. Empty. I looked underneath. No Eliot.

Turning to go back to the house, I spotted the listing wooden shed sitting several yards behind the farmhouse. Small indentations showed on the lawn. Footsteps? The new snowfall made it hard to tell. It took every ounce of courage I possessed to walk across the backyard, circling around a massive oak tree whose few remaining leaves rustled menacingly in the light wind, and approach the outbuilding.

The door was ajar, and although a crescent moon helped illuminate the area, I couldn't see much inside. I edged the door open farther with my foot. Still standing outside, I shined my cell phone flashlight around the small interior, which smelled like rotting mulch, hoping to spot Eliot curled up on the dirt floor.

I shrieked when I saw a pair of glowing eyes peeking out from a pile of rusted machinery, then the creature skittered away. "Just a mouse," I told myself, fighting to control my breathing, and continued to sweep the light around the shed.

I caught sight of something, but it took a couple seconds for the message to get to my brain. That bunch of rags I saw in the corner was not an errant pile of laundry.

It was Bernice.

Tears stung my eyes, and I rushed over and kneeled by

the cold, cold bed of the Dragon Lady, who would terrorize the town no more. She was wearing clothes I had seen her in before, a dark cardigan over a white blouse, a cast peeking out on her right arm, black skirt, and a pair of dirty slippers on her feet.

I gently touched her shoulder, sending a prayer out for her safe passage.

Back in the house, I reached for the landline phone on the kitchen wall, my hand trembling, my mind flashing back to that horrible day when I found the body of my dear Drew. Bernice's worldly troubles were at an end, but I knew my troubles might just be beginning. The police would have lots of questions, and experience had taught me that even the innocent would know no rest.

2

The paramedic, her brown hair pulled into a no-nonsense bun, sat near me on an old overstuffed chair in Bernice's living room. I huddled in the matching chair, my black wool coat hugged tightly to my body. A man who had earlier introduced himself as Detective Maccini returned from his squad car, carrying an oversized thermal bag. He called it his "emergency kit." He pulled Styrofoam cups and a large thermos jug from the bag, poured three cups of coffee, and set two of them on the stand between me and the watchful medic.

"Are you sure you don't want AnnMarie to take you to the hospital?" he asked again, peering down at me through unfashionable bifocals. "You're probably suffering from shock. We can have someone drive your car back to town."

I reached out a shaky hand and picked up the coffee, appreciating the heat of the cup, then shook my head no. "Thanks for this," I said. "I'll be okay. I just need to get warm. And figure out how to tell Sarah her mom is dead. And her cat is missing." I tried to blink away another round of tears, then decided it might be best to just go ahead and cry. The police like signs of grief.

"A cat? Indoor cat? Huh. What's it look like?" Maccini asked.

"Eliot, he's pretty big. And yes, an indoor cat with black and brown markings. His collar has a bell on it."

Maccini nodded, got up, and walked into the kitchen, where I could hear people moving around, opening cupboard doors and drawers. Someone had managed to unlock the door leading to Sarah's apartment, and footsteps sounded overhead. The detective held a murmured conversation with someone, then returned, settling on one end of a dark green sofa. He sipped his coffee, and lights from an ambulance and another county cop car parked outside splashed his face with color. In his heavy corduroys and flannel shirt, he looked more like a stressed out, overworked farmer than a police officer, and he sounded more like a concerned grandfather.

"We'll try to reach her soon," Maccini said. "This is going to be hard on her, she's lived with her mom for years. I hate these calls."

He leaned forward and softened his voice even more, as if this were a chummy conversation between friends. "I know this is difficult," he said, "but can you think of any reason Bernice would wander out in this weather? Was it common for the cat to go outside? Would Bernice go hunting for it, especially without her shoes? And was she taking any medicine that would leave her foggy? Was she depressed about anything?"

I shrugged my shoulders. "I didn't really know her that well, it was all a business relationship ..." I trailed off, exhaustion and cold and the whole weight of the evening's horror hitting me hard.

I saw AnnMarie glance over at Maccini, who apparently got the unspoken message. "I think we're done here for now," he said. "You need to get home and get some sleep if you can. I'll give you a call tomorrow, and on Tuesday you can come by headquarters and we'll prepare your statement: when you saw or talked to Bernice last, what you did tonight, that type of thing. Might help if you write some things down while they're still fresh in your mind."

He swallowed a final slug of coffee. "We'll take care of the rest. And don't worry, we'll keep looking for the cat."

3

Some Alleton shop owners, including Waves End owners Frank and Justin, took Monday as their day of rest, so downtown was on the quiet side when I finally made it there after a few hours of fitful sleep. I walked around my shop, trailing my fingers over half-empty shelves, picking up and putting down papers, longing for work to keep me busy. I desperately wanted to call Raelynn, my beloved aunt who had seen me through many of life's bumps, both molehills and mountains, but she was with her husband and their twin granddaughters on a Disney cruise and wouldn't be back until Saturday.

My store was called Bathing Beauty, the name doing double duty because the business I'd bought from Bernice in October offered hats, flip flops, sunscreen, and other handy items for beachgoers in late spring and all through summer, and lush body care products for use in the bath and shower all year round, plus a few fun items to capture the tourists' fancy. It needed some upgrades, generally with its product line and online presence.

Bernice and Sarah ran the store through Christmas, offering major close-out deals. I worked at the store during the holiday rush, learning the ins and outs of retailing, and took possession at the end of the year. The grand re-opening was set for early February, and things so far were moving smoothly.

"You can do it," I thought, channeling Aunt Raelynn's go-getter, no-excuses attitude. But I wasn't sure. There was so much I didn't know about running a store. Sarah was going to stay on as assistant manager, but now she had a funeral to plan and who knew how much work to do settling her mom's estate.

I kicked aside an empty box and was startled by a knock at the shop's door. I lifted the shade covering the front door's window and saw Frank, bundled in a warm fleece jacket and holding a paper bag and cardboard coffee caddy. "Lauren, Lauren," he said as he entered, setting the breakfast items on an empty counter and passing over the tea he'd brought for me. "I am so sorry. Heard the news about Bernice. How are you? Have you talked to Sarah yet? Are you okay? What did the police say? What can I do?"

Apparently, news does travel fast in small towns. That shouldn't have surprised me. Frank was the leader of the town's small business association and seemed to know everyone. He and Justin had owned Waves End for almost 15 years, specializing in photographic watercolors, funky modern sculpture, and all types of wall art. Or what Frank like to call "cool art for cold cash."

"This," I said, pointing to the homemade potato doughnuts he pulled from the sack. "And make sure the painter you selected finishes the outside sign in time. And no, I haven't talked to Sarah yet and I don't know if she's returned from Tennessee and I don't really know what to do or say to her and I have no idea what the police are saying but I have to go to the station to meet with Detective Maccini tomorrow and …," I ran out of breath and threw my arms around Frank for a hug.

We had become almost instant friends last October, when I made the rounds of the town's many shops and galleries, talking to owners and trying to decide whether to put in a bid on Bernice's store. "A Florida girl!" Frank said when I introduced myself. "In need of winter's cleansing cold. I like it." He treated me to lunch several times when I came back to town to sign paperwork after Bernice accepted my bid, filling me in on Alleton's history and popular hangouts and political issues, such as the continuing battle over assigned parking spaces, and giving me a sense of what to expect when summer arrived and tourists overran the town and jammed the nearby beach.

"If someone dares to park in the alley behind your store, call the police right away. Those spots are reserved for shop owners, and it's the one time you need to get tough with the customer base. 'Cause if someone takes your spot, you're outta luck."

He also invited me into what I thought of as his Alleton inner circle, several local merchants who formed something of a loose-knit family. Sarah and Bernice were part of the group, which may explain why I had been included. After all, I was the town newbie and had done nothing to earn a place in the circle. But if Frank gave his approval, that appeared to be all that was needed. So instead of lots of lonely nights, I had a set of friends, or, if they weren't true friends yet, at least friendly acquaintances, to spend time with.

Frank didn't ask a lot of personal questions, didn't want to know my life story or the reason I would want to move a thousand miles to set up shop in a Midwestern coastal town. He accepted the brief history I had prepared for those who asked. My husband had died unexpectedly about two years ago, I needed a fresh start, I was looking for franchise opportunities when a Florida snowbird had told me about a store for sale in the Michigan arts colony, and I craved work that would feed my entrepreneurial soul.

What I didn't share was that my parents, my brother, Greg, and my aunt Raelynn convinced me that leaving Florida and the nasty swirl of unfounded rumors about my involvement in Drew's death might be the best thing I could do for my mental health. And there was one other secret I never shared with anyone.

"Oh, sweet pea," Aunt Raelynn had said through tears as we sat in her beauty salon a few months earlier, "I don't want you to go, but you don't deserve this. Thirty is too young to live under such a dark cloud. And I'll come visit and be only a phone call away."

She had given me a long, critical look. "And while you're here, how about I give you a new look first — I always thought you'd look great as an auburn-haired vixen. Offset your pale skin and deep brown eyes." That was Aunt Raelynn, offering positive suggestions to counteract negative events. She had been a life-saving crutch for me when Drew died, always there to listen, to hug me when I cried, to convince me that life was still worth living.

"So, you need to talk to the police again," Frank said, interrupting my wandering thoughts. Even though he hadn't pressed me for details about my life in Florida, he wasn't going to give me a pass on my first-person view of the death of an Alleton business owner. That was sure to be a prime topic of conversation around town.

"Just to sign a witness statement," I said between bites of doughnut. "I can't add much, and they don't want to hear about how scary that evening was for me. Alone in a big house on a dark and cold night and thinking Freddy Krueger or some other movie nightmare was going to jump out from a closet and then finding poor Bernice …" I shuddered.

Frank pulled a folded paper out of his shirt pocket.

"Okay, let's talk about something less scary. This how the artist plans to update the Bathing Beauty sign, bring it into the 21st century. Check it out."

I reached over and traced the colored pencil sketch with my index finger but couldn't get my mind on business. "I wonder if Sarah would be in the mood to talk to you about this in a few days. She has a better sense of this place than I do."

"Maybe," Frank said. "You'll have to wait and see." He held a finger to his lips. "Keep in mind what I said. Now that her mom is dead, Sarah might be even angrier about not getting the shop. She might not be a friend of yours."

About 10 minutes after Frank left, the shop door opened again, letting in a blast of cold wind and the sound of a revving car.

"Hey," said Kylie Herron, the town's social media expert and youngest entrepreneur, "you need to lock this, or strange people looking to sell you their services might intrude." Evie, her niece, followed, looking cute in a bunny-eared hat.

Without asking whether I had time to talk, Kylie pulled off her coat and dumped it on a side counter, then helped Evie with her jacket. She settled Evie on a low counter, pulled a book out of her laptop bag, and handed her the paperback Dr. Seuss. Evie pointed at the doughnuts farther down on the counter.

Kylie's eyes lit up at Evie's discovery. "Frank's famous potato doughnuts? Are you sharing?"

I nodded. "Better someone else eats a few, otherwise I'll finish the entire batch."

"Don't tell your mom about this," Kylie whispered to Evie as she handed her niece one small bite of the treat. Evie, looking serious, nodded her head in agreement. The two shared black hair, but that's where the resemblance ended. Kylie's pixie cut accentuated hazel eyes and an olive complexion, while Evie's long swoop framed her light golden skin and dark eyes. Of Chinese descent, Evie had been adopted as an infant, and Kylie frequently was her babysitter. Evie, as usual, looked wan; I had heard the four-year-old was undergoing treatment for some type of blood disorder.

I wasn't getting a lot of work done but was happy with the interruption. Kylie, with her exuberance, and Evie, with her childish wonder, might, like Frank, help brush away some of the previous evening's darker memories. Besides, so many of the shop owners I had met were in their late 40s and 50s, and it was nice to talk with someone closer to my age. In fact, the raven-haired doll with the interesting style choices — I had heard that Kylie liked to shop at an upscale boutique in Chicago that featured vintage clothes, but today she had paired jeans with a cardigan embroidered with what looked to be either misshapen zucchini or pickles — was still in her 20s. She was a good example of a successful millennial.

"I heard about Bernice, but I'm not here to bring that up," Kylie announced, then took a good look around. "You got any tea here? Even coffee? Organic hot chocolate? That'd be good for Evie. If not, you need a Keurig or a Ninja, I like that one because of the name, but Keurig is really the better choice. I can get you a fabulous wholesale deal on one, even better than the online price." She wrinkled her nose. "Just one of my many side jobs."

I laughed and realized I hadn't been doing much of that lately. "You have a sale there, Kylie. I've just been stopping at the coffee shop down the street for a chai latte, but a ready-set-go hot beverage machine sounds like a good addition to this place."

"Speaking of," Kylie said, "what I really want to sell you is my expertise. I checked online, and this place has zero presence. None. Nada. Zippo. What's with that?"

I cut her off before Kylie could launch into her sales pitch. "I'm holding off on all that until the logo is finished. And I still need to decide on some new product lines. Those are on my list of things to talk about with Sarah, and I don't know when that will happen."

"Cutting it close, aren't you? Can you open in early February?" Kylie wiggled her fingers at me. "Okay, I get the message. No sale today. But I'll go ahead and work up a possible website home page, gratis. You and Sarah can decide what you think and only pay if you use it."

She gave me a sharp look. "One other thing. What gives with you, Lauren? No Facebook, Twitter, LinkedIn, Instagram, blah blah blah. Do you even exist? Are you in witness protection?"

I stood up straighter, hoping my face hadn't revealed my dismay. Before I could respond, however, she shrugged and said, "Well, we all have our secrets."

Then the cheerleader was back, bouncing up to put on her coat, outfitting Evie again in her jacket and bunny hat. At the door, she turned, bent down, and whispered to Evie, who offered a shy "Bye-bye."

"Bye, sweetie," I said, then blinked when I saw Kylie lift her cell phone, aim it my way, and take a quick photo.

"I'll work up a killer online presence for you," Kylie said. "Again, no charge unless you decide you want to use it. Ta-ta!" And away she went, leaving me speechless and a little afraid.

4

The two-story county police station was a no-frills place. The brick exterior at least gave it some warmth, but no attempt had been made to dress up the windows or doors. Then again, the all-business look was probably exactly what the cops wanted.

I walked in to the smell of burnt coffee and sound of the clicking of a computer keyboard and random bits of static from a police scanner. Detective Maccini came around the counter, wearing the warm, happy-to-see-you, how-can-I-help look I remembered from our Sunday night meeting. However, his standard police apparel of a long-sleeved navy shirt with black tie, navy pants, black shoes, and the requisite holster, gun, and handcuffs shouted "official business." He gave me a firm handshake then led the way to a bare-bones interview room. It was furnished with a metal table, a recorder sitting off to one side, a couple of ugly plastic chairs. The obligatory two-way mirror covered one wall. I wondered who might be watching on the other side.

"Thanks for coming by today. Can I get you a coffee?" he asked. "I'm having one, but I can't guarantee the quality." I demurred. Just entering the building had made me nervous, and I didn't need caffeine to add to my shakes.

"This will be easy," he told me as we took our places on the hard, plastic seats. "I'll turn on the recorder, ask you some questions about Sunday night, and when it's all done it will be typed up and you can sign it. But first, how are you feeling? That was a bad scare you had."

"I'm feeling mostly okay," I told him. "Talked to some friends, they made me feel better."

Maccini nodded. "Best thing. Talk it out. Glad to hear it."

"Before we start, can you tell me about Sarah? I haven't heard from her yet, don't know what to do."

The detective glanced at the closed file he'd placed on the table. "She drove back from Tennessee yesterday. She was pretty broken up, no surprise, but had a church friend come with her to the morgue last night. Same as you, probably needs some folks around. But really," he added, "not for me to say what you should do. So let's get on with your statement."

I could tell that he was more comfortable in his role as a cop than as a counselor but was sorry to see Maccini switch to a just-the-facts guy. Memories of the seemingly endless interrogation I went through in Tampa following Drew's death still had the power to anger me, although the bit of rationality I possessed in my grief-stricken haze reminded me that the police were only doing their job. And they weren't responsible for the Armageddon that resulted, much as I wanted to blame them. Today, sitting in a different interview room but surrounded by the same dirty industrial green walls that offered no promise of peace, I craved the understanding that was not forthcoming.

Detective Maccini turned on the recorder, intoned the time, date, his name and mine, and started by asking me to take him through what I had done on Sunday. I skipped telling him about the time I spent meditating, a helpful exercise I'd learned from my grief counselor in Florida. My recitation of an hour spent exercising to a fitness video and then working on an Excel spreadsheet until I left for Waves End around 6 p.m. was met with a blank stare.

"Bernice went to church Sunday morning," he said. "So 11 a.m. to late afternoon is what most interests me."

I fidgeted in the uncomfortable chair. I had no witnesses who could prove I was close to home in the afternoon and not committing a nefarious deed at Bernice's house. But I didn't understand what might have happened, what led Bernice in her slippers into the freezing weather. Could she have been looking for the cat? When I asked if the police had any more information, Maccini simply said, "Can't discuss that," and switched to asking what I noticed about the house, garage, and shed. He seemed particularly interested in what I had seen in the kitchen.

"You dropped off a plate of appetizers," he said, glancing at some notes, "but do you remember what else was on the counter?"

I closed my eyes, trying to bring back a picture of what I'd seen, but instead got a vision of Bernice, frail and cold and alone. "Sorry," I said. "I remember what wasn't there, Eliot, the cat, but a lot of the early stuff is mostly a blur." I also couldn't recall much of what I had said to him that terrible night and don't think I added anything of more interest, but Maccini seemed okay with the meager results.

"That's it," he said, as he disconnected the recorder. "Let me get this to the typist, won't take her long, then you can read it and sign. And are you sure about that coffee? We got cream, that helps."

"Sure," I said. "I'm not a big coffee drinker, but something warm before my drive back would be nice."

Maccini beamed, apparently happy I had accepted his cure-all.

An hour later, bad coffee drank, statement closely read

and signed, I handed the paperwork back to Maccini.

"Did Eliot ever show up?" I asked, crossing my fingers in a childlike wish for luck.

"Nope. No sign yet of the darn cat. Poor Sarah, she needed some better news." He led the way back to the station's front door. "We should be all set," he said, "but if anything else comes up, I'll be back in touch. And oh, the autopsy is scheduled for tomorrow."

"Autopsy?" I was taken aback. "I thought it was pretty clear how she died."

"To you and me, yeah. Poor dear froze to death. But she was only 75 years old, had no history of major health problems. The medical examiner wants to know more. Frankly, so do I. What led her to go outside in that weather? Who let the cat out? Ya gotta wonder."

5

Watching the hardy souls power walk near the icy edge of the Lake Michigan shoreline below my second-floor rented condo had quickly become part of my morning "mindful meditations." I was beginning to appreciate the beauty of the frozen north, even though my own occasional morning strolls on the yellow sand always left me chilled to the bone. How did people up here survive this winter stuff?

The condo didn't do a lot to warm me either. The owner, a professor away on sabbatical, went with black and white as his color scheme. I saw the hand of a high-end decorator at work, but the stark rooms didn't shout "welcome home" to me. I wondered if I would ever feel welcome anywhere again.

The buzz of my cell phone interrupted my early Wednesday morning reverie. I glanced at the caller ID and my heart did a little flip. It was Sarah. "It's so good to hear from you. How are you?" I held my breath. Would Sarah be angry with me for not calling her Sunday night, even though the police told me not to?

"Oh, Lauren, I'm so, so sorry about what you went through. The cops told me you were, that you found Mom. I can't, I can't begin to imagine how bad that was. Are you okay? Are, are you ..." Sarah's voice broke, and I heard muffled crying.

"Do you need a visitor? Can I come see you? I can bring

some breakfast and help with whatever you need."

"Would you? Do you mind? That would be so nice. I just, I really, I don't know, there's so much to do and the police are doing an autopsy today and I, I don't think I can stand the thought of that and, and …"

I spoke through the sound of Sarah's sobs. "I'm on my way."

* * *

In the light of day, the farmhouse appeared decrepit, not spooky. The paint was fading, the front porch steps were rotting, and a window shutter was missing, giving the old homestead the air of a listing drunk. As I once again parked against the garage door, the sight of the backyard shed gave me a chill that had nothing to do with the day's icy drizzle. It was probably for the best, I thought, that I was the one who found Bernice. If it had been Sarah, how could she possibly continue to live in this lonely, sagging, country dwelling? Even now, it had to be rough.

Sarah met me at the kitchen door, her eyes red from weeping. Still no Eliot. I didn't ask, just hugged her.

"Let's go upstairs to my apartment," Sarah said as she tried to get her sniffles under control. "Downstairs just reminds me of Mom and me lounging around playing cards and, and watching TV. I don't know if I'll ever be able to sit down here now."

Sarah, a tissue wadded in her left hand, led the way, and I followed with the bag of bagels I'd brought. I had never seen this part of the house before and was happy to have my curiosity satisfied. The top of the stairs gave way to a short hallway, with three doors on the left and only one to the right. Sarah opened the door on the right, walked into the room, and motioned for me to enter.

I almost gasped at the sight. The large room, probably

23

originally intended to serve as an attic, was furnished in what my limited knowledge of decor could only call country chic. A brown leather sofa and two plaid wingback chairs held pride of place in a conversation grouping, and a huge flat screen TV hung on the wall. The airy room, with its cute country accessories, sisal carpet, and muted earth tone walls looked inviting — and expensive.

Sarah gave me a rueful smile. "Different, huh? Mom didn't want to spend the money to, to update the downstairs, but genteel poverty is not the look I want. I do have my pride. And, and speaking of, I need to change. Can't talk to the funeral home people in these old sweats."

Against her "old sweats," my typical casual winter outfit of jeans, a long-sleeved T-shirt, and an oversized sweater made me look like her poor second cousin. I had yet to figure out how to look stylish while staying warm.

When Sarah left, I wandered around the space. This was another view of the person I had come to know only as a shop assistant, a divorced, childless, 50-something, slightly pudgy woman with lightly frosted hair who dressed in classic clothes and was always pleasant to be around. Her verbal tic of repeating words tended to get worse when she was nervous, but I barely paid attention to it anymore.

Some sort of mechanical bank sitting on top of a pine desk that overflowed with envelopes and papers caught my eye. While not my style of household accessories, I was taken by the cast iron pig sitting on a barrel, ready to accept a coin in the platter on his lap. I picked it up, trying to figure out how the pig accepted a coin. Maybe Sarah would demonstrate the trick.

"What are you doing?" I jerked back, surprised, my hip hitting the desk. "Just looking at the cute piggy bank," I said, turning to see Sarah walking toward me, her bloodshot eyes narrowed with anger. "I thought maybe you could show me how it works." I put the bank back and hurriedly gathered the papers that had slipped to the floor and handed them to Sarah.

"Oh, jeez, I'm sorry. You, it's just that you reminded me of when Mom, when she snooped through my stuff. That, that's why I finally put a lock on the door leading up here." Sarah stuffed the papers into one of the drawers and gave me a rueful smile. "Not your fault. I'm just, just a little on edge. I really am sorry."

"No need to apologize. I get it. But if you demonstrate how the pig picks up the coin, all is forgiven. And then let's have some bagels."

"It hasn't worked in ages," Sarah said. "It's silly, but I, I love this thing. My dad got it for me when I was a kid. When I look at it I remember how he would put a penny in it, and we would laugh and laugh at the action.

"I wish it still worked, but the lever in the back it, it broke off." She set the bank back on the desk. Although sad, her remembrance broke the tension in the room.

"I didn't know you had such a flair for interior design," I told her. "And maybe if you put your gift to work downstairs, you might feel comfortable there again." My grief-counseling skills were minimal, but I knew Aunt Raelynn would approve of my attempt to cast a positive light on what I could only see as a dreadful option. If Sarah said she planned on moving, I would have given her a positive pep talk.

"It's a career I once thought I should check out, but well, life, life happens, and plans change."

Frank's warning about Sarah came back to me. I hesitated then decided to take advantage of her current vulnerability. If she had plans that meant she was moving on and would not start a legal fight for ownership of what everyone had assumed would eventually be her store, I'd be glad to hear them. "You still could, you know. Looks like you already have the eye for it, and I bet there are classes you could take."

Sarah swept her arm around, encompassing the room. "I can do this but, but I'm no good at marketing myself. I can sell stuff to tourists, and I do a good job at it, you should know, but, but selling my expertise, selling myself," she paused, "it didn't work in my personal life so well, you know, so I don't have high hopes."

Despite Frank's warning, none of that sounded like a threat to my ownership of Bathing Beauty.

"I don't want to rush you," I said later, as I stood at the back door of the house, digging out my car keys, "but do you know when you want to come back to the store? I could use your help on some last-minute decorating and the look of our website and the new sign."

A small smile lit Sarah's face. "Oh, you didn't approve the sign yet? I so wanted to help with that. Maybe, perhaps early next week? Is, is that soon enough? It will be good to keep busy after the funeral." The happy look left her face at the mention of a funeral.

During the drive back to Alleton, I berated myself for my insensitive questioning. I also wondered why Sarah was so freaked when she saw me at her desk. That little incident reminded me of what Kylie had said: "We all have our secrets."

6

The lights in the Tomlinsons' Wooden Block, on a side street around the corner and several buildings down from Bathing Beauty, were on, even though the store closed the last three weeks of January. I made a quick detour there before going to my own shop. When I peered in the window, I saw Tami by a rear wall, shelving boxes of some merchandise, and I pounded on the door. Tami turned, then walked to the front when she saw me.

"Thought you were a customer wanting to look around," Tami said when she opened the door. "A big closed sign doesn't always mean a thing to some people. But come on in, I need a break." She wiped her hands on her baggy navy-blue sweatpants, leaving a trail of dust. "Want something to drink?"

"I'm good, thanks. What I do want is a favor. Sarah's busy with her mom's funeral, and I need to hire someone to help stock the inventory and paint the woodwork. Do you know if D.J. might be available?"

The mention of her son's name made Tami smile. The poor woman might have a bad marriage, but she and Dennis had a fine son to show for the pairing. D.J., who was working on a master's degree in chemical engineering, usually had January free, unless he was involved in a research project.

"He's doing something for Kylie right now, but he'll be

back in a couple hours," Tami told me. "I'll have him call you. Pretty sure he'd be happy to earn a little spare cash."

She sighed. "Sorry about what you went through with Bernice. That's awful. I'm also sorry you had to hear me and Dennis fight. I know you were at the January Doldrums gathering the other day, saw you peeking around the corner. Didn't mean to scare you off."

"Wasn't your fault, Tami. I was in a rush to get to Bernice's. Anyway, turns out I was too late." The memory of how I found her made me blink away tears.

"Ahh, you can't take the blame for that one. You was nice to her. Think of that." She twisted the bottom hem of her sweatshirt. "Don't feel bad about me neither. I'm a lot stronger than people give me credit for."

"Deal," I told her, and as I left Wooden Block, I thought of the times Aunt Raelynn and I would dance around her dining room table shouting the words to "I Will Survive," one of my aunt's favorite songs, an old disco hit by Gloria Gaynor that celebrated the power of women.

I made it back to Bathing Beauty just as a delivery van showed up with the first round of my new inventory. Boxes and boxes of private label organic body care products, all with environmentally friendly packaging. That had been Sarah's suggestion. The shop's former product line hadn't been selling well, and she suggested the change might help.

"They are pricier," she'd told me, "and my mom didn't want to put out the cash, but the old way wasn't working anymore." I had run the numbers on what had been selling at the store the past three years and decided the bigger outlay was worth the risk. Sarah was thrilled that I took her advice, and I was pleased that my research backed up her gut reaction to what the customers might want.

A knock on the shop door interrupted my whirlwind

attempt at unpacking boxes. The store was set to open in a little over four weeks, and I was starting to get nervous about meeting the time. Seeing Detective Maccini at the door, wearing a heavy leather jacket over dress blues, did nothing for my mental state.

When I opened the door, the officer handed me a carrier holding two cups of coffee. "Ms. Andrews, got a minute? I got coffee."

I motioned to the stacks of boxes. "I am kind of busy, but sure, I have a little time."

Maccini pulled off his jacket, and he and I each took one of the chairs I'd previously pulled into the front of the shop from my minuscule office. He surprised me with a big smile. "Good news! That cat, what's the name? Eliot? Strange name. Anyway, one of my officers was just at the farmhouse, taking pictures, checking distances, all that kind of stuff, and when he was done he saw this big ole cat sitting by the kitchen door. Probably wanted to be fed. He knocked on the door, I mean the officer, not the cat, and when Sarah saw what the officer was holding it apparently was like the second coming. So, the cat is back."

I let out a whoop of glee. "Oh, good! I was there this morning, and it was too sad. This doesn't make up for losing her mom, but it has to make Sarah feel better."

My euphoria lasted about a minute. "Got a bit of not-so-good news, too," Maccini said. "Some tests came back. Seems Mrs. Mullins ingested a lot of sleeping pills. But we didn't find anything like that in her house. Which means I gotta check. Do you know if she ever took those things?"

The friendly counselor was starting to look a bit more like a police officer. I frowned and shook my head. "Bernice never mentioned sleep problems to me. I do know she was an early riser. When we were working out the terms of the business deal, she'd sometimes call me at 6:30 in the morning, but she always sounded bright and together. Don't sleeping pills leave people tired, even in the morning?" I realized I was talking too much, so I picked up the coffee cup and took a sip.

That wasn't the end of the detective's revelations.

"Here's a couple other things. Remember my asking what you saw on the kitchen counter? You said you didn't remember, but you put those appetizers you brought right next to a plate of cookies."

His "You said you didn't remember" statement took me aback, his wording making it sound like he didn't believe me.

"Well, we tested a bunch of stuff we found in the kitchen, including that plate of cookies. Odd thing. A couple of those cookies included something extra. Appears the pastry chef added liquid sleeping medicine to the recipe. But not to all of them. Huh.

"Sarah says her mom was not a baker. And we found no sign that Bernice made those cookies." He drank some coffee and cocked his head at me.

My unease was quickly turning into fear. First Maccini asks a seemingly innocent question about Bernice taking sleeping pills, then he drops the news about the cookies. I sat taller in the chair, looked him straight in the eye, and hoped I looked interested in his remarks but not the least bit guilty. And now I understood his interest in my whereabouts during the day on Sunday.

"You know, Lauren, after the tox screen but before we tested the cookies, we didn't know if we were looking at an accidental overdose, a suicide or, well, worst case, somebody wanted poor Bernice dead."

He paused for a few seconds, just staring at me. "Now

we know. Huh. Think of that. Someone enjoyed cookies and tea with Bernice, ate the safe ones and gave her the poisoned ones. Not sure how she ended up outside. But we do know one thing for sure.

"It was murder."

The world seemed to shrink to hold just the two of us: Maccini leaning back in his chair, his arms crossed over his belly, still gazing at me, and me, speechless and horrified by the thought of a poisonous soul deliberately taking Bernice's life. I wanted to strike out at him, at anyone, wanted this nightmare to stop.

Maccini made the first move. He reached into his shirt pocket and pulled out a small notebook and pen, now fully a police officer.

"Got more questions now, things I didn't know to ask when I got your statement." His manner was calm, the opposite of what I was feeling. "People around here called Bernice the Dragon Lady, and it seems lots of people disliked her. You did a major business deal with her. I'd like to hear about that, maybe see some paperwork, get a feel for your history with her."

His words jarred me from my speechless state. I held up a hand. "Whoa, give me a minute." Just as I had in the county police's interview room, I flashed back to the time a police officer in Florida had grilled me about my relationship with Drew. That detective didn't seem to care that I was so heartbroken over my husband's death I could barely put a coherent sentence together. The memory brought tears to my eyes, but when I finally looked over at Maccini, I was beyond crying.

"Do I need a lawyer?"

Now it was Maccini's turn to look surprised. "Well, I'm not accusing you or anything" — I could hear the unspoken word "yet" — "so I'm not sure why you would ask that, maybe you been watching way too many cop shows on TV. But hey, if you feel the need, go for it."

I thought for a few seconds, then gave him what I hoped was a defiant glare. "I didn't know then that people called her the Dragon Lady, but I think that's only because she spoke her mind. We reached what we both thought was a fair deal, and my lawyer worked out the details."

I pulled a business card and pen out of my purse, checked my cell phone for a number, then carefully printed a name and the number on the back of the card.

"Here's the name and contact info of the business attorney I used. I'll let him know he can speak to you. Feel free to call and ask your questions." I handed the card to Maccini and pointed to the door. "Now I'd like you to leave." The detective stared at me, his face unreadable, got up, put on his coat, and walked over to and out the shop's front door, letting in a blast of winter's unrelenting chill.

I got up, too, and when he reached the sidewalk, I leaned out the doorway and called his name. He looked back. "Detective Maccini, two more things. Thank you for the coffee. And here's a tip. I prefer tea. A good investigator should have known that."

Maccini lifted a gloved hand in a salute, turned, and continued down the sidewalk. I closed the front door and beat my fist against it.

"Stupid, stupid, stupid," I berated myself out loud. Why was I alienating the police? My anger against Maccini's insinuations was mixed with my fear that a stone-cold killer was out there, and it might be someone I knew.

7

I sped to my SUV after Thursday's funeral service for Bernice so I could get out of the lot before the line of cars started the slow trip to the cemetery. Earlier, I'd told a weeping Sarah I was skipping the post-funeral lunch to do some work at the shop but would be at that evening's private wake.

"I'm, I'm looking forward to being with friends," she said. "My only remaining relative is a distant cousin, Edward, and he and I barely know each other, so there won't, I won't have any family gathering."

The news that Bernice had been murdered, had eaten some cookies laced with a sleeping aid, had caused quite a buzz before the services started. But it was a solemn occasion, so people were deferential, talking in low tones. The minister conducting the memorial service did not call attention to the terrible fact of murder, only saying that Bernice had been called "before her time."

Frank and Justin were opening Waves End for the invitation-only wake after their gallery's 6 p.m. closing. "Bernice was a Dragon Lady," Justin, whose quiet demeanor and black-frame-glasses hipster look offered a good foil to Frank's occasional theatrics, told me when he issued the invitation, "but she was one of us. And we owe it to Sarah."

When I arrived at my shop, D.J. was already there. He

had used the key I had dropped into the Wooden Block's mail slot the previous evening after he'd accepted my offer of employment over the phone. He'd skipped the funeral, and, since he didn't bring it up, I guessed he hadn't heard the news about Bernice's death now being classified a homicide. I didn't say anything either, not in the mood to discuss the tragic development.

D.J., wearing an old pair of jeans and ragged sweatshirt, had clearly been busy. The smell of paint hung in the air and a jumble of empty boxes covered half the floor space. Several counters held row after row of creams and lotions.

Apparently, the young Tomlinson hadn't inherited his dad's surly outlook on life. As I grabbed various bottles and put them in their proper slots, I found his cheeriness a welcome break from that morning's sorrowful event. And he worked hard. I tried not to think about the short time left before the store's grand opening — less than a month away — and Maccini's implied suspicion hanging over my head. Damn the man.

"What do you think? Is this a good look for me?" D. J. was wearing one of the floppy hats that Sarah had said were a hit with beachgoers. With his model-perfect, square-jawed look, which didn't appear to come from either Tami or Dennis, just about anything would look good on the tall, well-toned 23-year-old.

"I think it's a bit too early for summer merchandise," I said, grinning at him, "and deep purple just isn't your color. Before you leave, why don't you haul those empty boxes to the recycling bin? And oh, not to be too nosy, which I am about to be, but I heard you and Kylie were dating."

"That's going nowhere," he said, looking inside one of the boxes as if it might magically hold a better answer. "Mom said I could learn something from her work ethic, but, I don't know. Even when we're together, she's on her phone or leaving in a rush or spending the day in Chicago. I thought it could be serious, then, poof, suddenly she pulled away. Guess work won out over me."

He sighed. "I shouldn't be so mean. Kylie spends a lot of time with Evie. That poor girl's pretty sick, needs a lot of care, and Kylie does love her niece."

D.J. might be protesting a bit too much, since he was hard at work on his chemical engineering degree and seemed to focus on his own future, too. "Well, things will work out or they won't," I said, then inwardly groaned at my weak relationship advice. Where was Aunt Raelynn when I really needed her, which was always. "So from what I've been hearing, it seems like you have no plans to go into the retail business. Your parents are probably disappointed."

"Yeah, running a toy store isn't my thing." D.J. slit open another box. "I get that Mom and Dad are unhappy about that, but it's not the life for me. Besides, if they want to give it up, I'm sure they could sell the business."

"They been talking about that?"

"Nah." D.J. laughed. "Dad jokes to Mom that he's worth his weight in gold, but only if he's dead, 'cause he's got a huge insurance policy." He grimaced. "Shoot, shouldn't have said that. Dad would be furious if he knew I blabbed, and you know how he gets."

I did know. But D.J.'s chatter reminded me of how my life had turned out. I looked around at the business I owned. Life insurance could be a lifesaver for those left behind.

8

The upstairs apartment of Frank and Justin's Waves End gallery was crowded with people gathered for the wake for Bernice, soft jazz lending a soothing vibe to the event. Frank, wearing a plain apron in deference to the occasion, handed me a glass of something orange when I came around the corner from the kitchen into the main living area. "My special drink for the grieving," he said, "a touch of sweetness. Sarah needs that. Still, her life might be better now that she's not under the Dragon Lady's thumb."

I gave him a startled look. "Shoot, listen to me," he said. "Didn't mean to imply anything. That was horrible news about Bernice." He glanced around, but no one was nearby. "I can't get over the idea that there might be a killer around. Maybe even someone I know."

We both surveyed the people filling the apartment, people who had welcomed me to the community when I bought Bernice's store. The idea that one of them would kill someone also seemed impossible to me.

I did, however, want to clear up something. "Frank, what is the deal with you and Sarah? Every time you mention her, you don't have much good to say. I thought you liked her."

"Oh, I like everyone, that's a fact. But Sarah always seems to be planning some nefarious deed." He gasped. "No, no, no, not murder. Damn, need to be careful what I say. But she can be so freaking secretive, and you know me,

I hate secrets. I'm pretty sure she's hiding something. Several months ago, she asked Justin about what lawyer we used when we arranged to open this gallery. What would she want a lawyer for unless she was trying to get her name on Bernice's store? And we know that didn't work out."

His news gave me pause, but in all my dealings with Sarah, I had never seen a sign of her wanting to take over the store. I had to agree that she was on the secretive side, witness her reaction when I knocked the papers off her desk.

Frank lifted his glass of orange whatever-it-was in a toast to me. "Pay no attention to me. I'm upset. All the merchants here are close, and Bernice being murdered is too terrible for words."

Unlike their subdued behavior at that morning's funeral services, people at the wake seemed, if anything, a bit giddy. It was a little weird, but it appeared Frank's special orange stuff was doing its job. And I must have missed the meeting, but a group decision seemed to have been made to ignore the manner of Bernice's death. The normally surly Dennis, looking sloppy in oversized, faded brown corduroy pants and a dark green sweater covered with pills, was laughing at something social media guru Kylie said to him, and Justin, usually reserved, was chatting easily to a circle of Alleton merchants. Even Sarah occasionally smiled, although I also saw her blink away tears as people would give her a hug and talk quietly.

"Hey Tami," I said, approaching the woman who was standing by herself. "I really want to thank you for telling D.J. about my need for some help this week. He's priceless."

Tami smiled, a rare occurrence for her. "Yeah, he is a gem, even if I do say so myself. He don't want to end up running Wooden Block, a shame for Dennis and me, but you won't find a better worker."

"I've heard mixed reports of how the holiday season went for some of the shops here," I said. "How did the toys go?"

"We did good," Tami said. She pointed at D.J., who was standing nearby, talking to an attractive blonde, and glowed with maternal pride. "Our sales were always best on the days D.J lent a hand. Soccer moms love that boy." We both laughed.

As the wake continued, Justin constantly brought out more appetizers, Kylie offered drink refills, and Frank entertained the group with his stories about some of the gallery's more outrageous artists. Even Dennis chimed in, telling about one of his toy shop's obnoxious customers. "This woman got mad because we didn't have a Lego set that featured a kid with a mullet. Her nephew was into that, and she wanted him to know she thought it was cool. Tami heard what was going on and came over right quick, knew I was about to lose my cool."

The only time the laughter stopped was when Sarah raised her glass to the party-goers. "You are all so sweet," she said, "and, and everyone has always been so nice to me. Frank, Justin, this means, this means so much to me. All of you, thank you for coming and for being at the funeral today. I, I know my mom would have appreciated your presence." She faltered, and Frank quickly put his arm around her. "You know we're all here for you," he said. "You can count on us."

Her speech seemed to mark a farewell, both to Bernice and to the party. Kylie offered to escort Sarah to her car, and once they were out the door the moratorium on the discussion of murder ended. I wandered around the room, eavesdropping on conversations.

"I still can't believe it. Who would want to kill a nice lady like Bernice?" one older gentleman said. I guess the idea of not speaking ill of the dead meant no one would refer to her as the Dragon Lady, at least for a while.

"You know, I hate to say it," I heard someone else say, although she didn't hate it enough to stay quiet, "but I wonder if the police have checked on Sarah. Was she really away on vacation?"

No one paid much attention to me until a woman named Natalie, owner of one of the town's three clothing boutiques and a fan of gaudy costume rings, reached out and tightly grasped my hand. "I'm so glad to see you're freshening up Bathing Beauty," she said. "It looks bad for the town to have empty or run-down shops, which happened during that terrible recession. Poor Bernice was struggling, and so were a lot of us.

"To make it worse, she and Sarah were having terrible arguments." She let go of my hand and took a sip of her punch. "That girl wanted Bernice to dump some of the cheaper product lines and invest in high-end stuff. I ask you, if people couldn't afford the cheap stuff, how could they pay for the expensive stuff?"

I murmured a noncommittal reply. I didn't tell her that Sarah had made the same suggestion to me, and my own research had shown that she was on the right track. Even during the recession, the idea probably would have worked. Sarah knew her customer base and figured out that the well-to-do still could afford luxurious body care products. They may have stopped buying high-end shoes and purses and designer clothes, and Natalie had no doubt felt that pinch, but $10 extra for private-label botanicals wouldn't break their golden piggy banks. That, at least, was my not-so-expert opinion.

"Well," Natalie said, "I wasn't surprised when Bernice decided to sell and didn't hand the store to Sarah. People thought it was a terrible way to treat her daughter, but that Bernice, she had standards, and I know she was afraid Sarah would drive the shop into deep debt.

"You wouldn't know this, but when Sarah's then-husband took off with all the money in their accounts, it was Bernice who gave her a place to live. People forget that. So you can't fault her. At least Bernice protected her investment. Don't know about the will, but I bet Sarah did just fine."

Natalie, apparently out of gossip, nodded at me and marched off in the direction of the bar. Well, one mystery solved, I thought. I didn't know whether Sarah or Bernice had been in the right, but now I knew why Sarah didn't get a chance to buy Bathing Beauty. Ah, family dynamics.

The wake was winding down, and several people were collecting their coats. A few feet from me, I saw Dennis, heavy winter jacket in hand, waving to Tami. He looked a little unsteady, and I hoped he wasn't driving. Someone needed to intervene. Then I saw Tami, keys clutched in her hand, and relaxed. She obviously knew better than to let him take the wheel. As the two moved toward the stairs, Dennis dropped his coat. He looked around, appearing confused. He took another step, then staggered against Tami, who almost lost her footing. Justin, standing nearby to bid farewell to the departing guests, reached over to steady her.

Dennis took another step, gave another look at his wife, and collapsed to the floor. Justin, who had moved from Tami's side in a fruitless attempt to stop Dennis's fall, bent down and cradled Dennis's head. He leaned over, his ear close to Dennis's nose and mouth. The guests grew quiet, watching as Justin gave Dennis a couple small shakes.

Finally, Justin lifted his head and looked around the room.

"He's not breathing! He's not breathing! Someone call 911!" While Justin pleaded for help, several people pulled out their cell phones, punching in the digits. Tami dropped to her knees and grabbed Dennis's hand. D.J. raced over, and he took his mother's other hand, his eyes on his father.

Kylie, who had earlier returned to the wake, rushed up and roughly pushed Justin away from Dennis. "I can do CPR," she cried. "I can do it!"

She knelt beside Dennis, her face intense. "Get back! I got this."

After several minutes of Kylie compressing Dennis's chest, stopping on occasion to breathe into his mouth, then continuing with the compressions, Justin tried to pull her from the unresponsive man.

"No!" she yelled, knocking Justin aside. "I have to keep doing it. It's not too late."

9

When the medics arrived, one of them bodily lifted Kylie away from Dennis, while the other bent down to continue the CPR. She didn't, however, but instead looked up and flashed Kylie a smile.

"It's okay," she said, "you did a perfect job. He's breathing."

Tami let out a shriek, D.J. reached over and hugged her, and everyone else in the room took a deep breath, as though breathing for Dennis. Kylie hugged the other medic, who gently returned the hug then turned his attention back to Dennis.

The medics didn't put Dennis on a stretcher and move him until they were satisfied that he was breathing at a steady rate. They told Tami she could go along in the ambulance. D.J., face so pale it looked like he would be the next to collapse, told his mom he'd take the car and meet her at the hospital.

Once they were gone, those of us remaining helped Frank and Justin clean up by gathering dishes, picking up bits of trash, rinsing glassware. When that was done, we all joined the hosts at the bar and dipped into the punch bowl, seeking a fortifying nightcap.

"Thought I was going to have a heart attack myself," Frank said, rubbing his forehead with his apron. "I'll go to the hospital now and send out a message with an update. But Den's a strong guy, he should be okay."

* * *

The next morning, I was happy to see that several cars were parked on the streets of downtown Alleton, maybe a sign that customers were still in a buying mood. People bundled against the cold hurried into the few open shops, trying to avoid the chilly wind. The boutique across the street from Bathing Beauty, one that specialized in designer clothing for fashionable women of a certain age, was packed with bargain-hunters for its annual January sale. And Frank's latest message had good news. Dennis had survived through the night.

D.J. was supposed to meet me that morning to continue stocking inventory, but his father's brush with death meant he was keeping his mom company at the hospital. Frank's message had said Dennis was in the intensive care unit. I sighed and picked up a box cutter. The work had to be done, even though all I wanted to do was curl up at the condo with some hot tea and gaze out at the frozen expanse of Lake Michigan.

Two hours into the job, my focus directed on unpacking and shelving various products, I was startled when someone pounded on the shop door. I went over, lifted the shade, saw Kylie standing here, and quickly let her in.

The young woman's face was drawn. She dropped the two boxes she was carrying on the front counter. "Your Keurig," she told me, her usually perky voice low, "and some K-cups. I didn't know what to do today and thought maybe some errands would make me feel better."

I gave her a tight hug. "Oh, Kylie, you were fabulous last night. We all thought he was dead, but you wouldn't give up. You should be celebrating this morning, you saved

43

Dennis's life."

"Yeah," Kylie said as she removed her long, wool coat. "But it's not good. I stopped by the hospital, and D.J. told me his dad is still in bad shape, he might die. I don't know what I'll do if he dies. It's not right. I tried so hard. He can't die."

She sniffed and then pointed at the Keurig box. "Can we set that up? I need some hot chocolate. I don't know what else to do. Oh, Lauren, it's all so awful."

We busied ourselves with the coffee maker. I went back to the office area and returned with some cups, and she made herself hot chocolate while I went with tea, both of us relaxing a bit as the smell of chocolate spread through the room. Eventually, Kylie reached into her laptop bag and pulled out some papers, spreading them out on a nearby counter.

"I brought by some samples of my plan for your website. You want to look? It would take my mind off last night."

I was impressed with the sketches, how in all of them Kylie had managed to portray Bathing Beauty as the place that could serve "a woman for all seasons."

"This is my favorite," I said, pointing to the more subdued of the three options. It featured a lake scene in the background and a woman who looked to be in her early 20s, wearing a bathing suit and one of the shop's trademark hats, standing on the beach, stretching her arms to the sky, an Adirondack chair nearby. A change of the lake view for each season and adding warmer clothes to the celebrating woman, Kylie pointed out, would make the sketch work year round.

We discussed the drawing for several minutes. I kept waiting for Kylie to mention my lack of a personal social media presence, but the subject never came up.

Kylie, whose downcast demeanor had been replaced by her typical perky attitude, checked her phone again. "I need to get going," she said. "I want to go back to the hospital and see if D.J. might want to talk. Poor guy. His dad can be a jerk and he makes Tami's life hell, but still, the thought of losing your dad is scary, even if you have to wonder sometimes if it might be for the best."

"It's probably too soon to know," I said, "but have you heard about what caused Dennis's collapse?"

"D.J. didn't seem to know," Kylie said as she fixed another cup of hot chocolate, her rush to get to the hospital apparently forgotten. The poor girl seemed to feel the need to talk. "He told me once his dad had some sort of heart problem, but I wasn't paying that much attention."

"So," I said, "how are things between you and D.J., if you don't mind my asking."

Kylie blinked and bit her lip. "Well, we're mostly friends, I guess you could say. He's busy with school, and I'm always running around trying to keep my business on track. I think we might have different long-term goals. And I noticed at the wake that he was spending a lot of time with that cute blonde. I don't know who she is, maybe a niece of Natalie's."

I didn't detect any spiteful jealousy. I also realized that D.J.'s side of the story might not have been completely correct. Sounded like both had priorities that didn't include a serious romance. Which was a shame, they seemed to be a good match. But I wasn't about to push romantic advice.

Kylie looked at her phone again, sighed, and pushed her second cup of chocolate away. "I really should go. Enjoy your coffee maker, the bill's inside the box. Since you like my idea, I'll come back in a day or two with the final designs that show the change of seasons. Sarah might like a look, too."

I turned off the front lights after Kylie left and headed to the tiny office area at the back of the shop. Enough with the interruptions. I sat at the office desk, closed my eyes for a second, and took some deep breaths. Then I scrolled down the list of contacts on my cell phone and clicked on one of the names. The phone rang several times, and I was about to give up when it was finally answered. I felt a sense of joy when I heard my brother Greg's voice.

"Egg!" I said, "Hey, it's Victoria, you got time to talk?" The "Egg" nickname was from the days when I, two years younger than Greg, couldn't quite pronounce his name.

"Don't call me that!" His familiar rejoinder did my heart good. "But yeah, I can talk. It's good to hear from you, Vic. I thought you had forgotten us."

I bit my tongue to keep from telling him that the phone worked both ways. And I knew that his "I can talk now" had nothing to do with how busy he was and everything to do with the fact that his wife, Carmen, wasn't nearby.

Carmen was Drew's sister, and it was at Greg and Carmen's wedding that I met Drew. He had just returned from his final deployment in Iraq. He was a groomsman, and I was a bridesmaid.

We were married a year later. Drew, honorably discharged from his military service but unable to forget about some of the nightmarish action he had faced, went back to his job as an electrician. I continued my work as a database analyst at the University of Tampa, a job I found less than exciting.

"You always wanted to start your own business," Drew told me once when we strolled along the Tampa Riverwalk, admiring the many people out promenading with their dogs. "That's cool. Think about it." He leaned over and gave me a quick kiss.

Two years later, I was a widow.

Carmen had not joined the chorus of those asking questions about Drew's death, but their cousin Raul's suspicion about my involvement put her in a tough spot. She stopped inviting me to some of her immediate family events. My brother told me he didn't agree with Carmen, he thought I should always be welcome. But Carmen, like Drew, had bouts of depression, and Greg was worried about an argument bringing on another episode in his pregnant wife.

The trouble for me started when Raul announced widely that he figured Drew's death had not been an accident and perhaps his widow knew more than she was telling. The accusation spread online, and soon I was being hounded by nasty messages and name-calling by anonymous trolls. Even worse, I was snubbed by some of Drew's friends and relatives, and even some of my friends began to act uncomfortable in my presence.

But for Carmen, Greg's wife and Drew's sister, to pull away from me, and for Greg not to take my side, had caused me the pain that drove me to begin searching for a life away for Florida, away from the friends and family I held dear.

Greg's voice interrupted my dismal reverie. "Did you get the latest picture I sent of Roberto? He's so big now. And he loved the toy horse barn you sent for his birthday. And are you loving the cold up there?"

I refrained from asking how Carmen had responded when the gift arrived, but apparently Roberto had received it, so that made me feel better. Roberto was a blood nephew to both Drew and me, and his presence made me feel as though something of Drew lived on.

"I did get the photo. Thank you for sending it. He is a

little chubby-face darling. And the cold is what one of the other retailers up here refers to as 'refreshing.' I have other words for it."

I hesitated, then decided to tell Greg what had prompted my call.

"Unfortunately, the cold isn't really my problem now." I took a deep breath and started in. "The woman whose shop I bought died a few days ago. I found her body. It was terrible." I heard Greg gasp. "She was murdered, Egg! She wasn't real popular, and she annoyed a lot of people, but she didn't deserve to die."

I hoped I sounded calm when I told him the rest of my news. "A police officer up here has started asking me lots of questions. He acts like he thinks I killed her."

My bald statement was met with a few seconds of silence.

"Vic, what the hell have you gotten yourself into?" Greg finally said. "Murder? Seriously? And what, you found her body?"

"I did, Egg, and it was, oh, I can't even tell you how awful it was. I wish you were here, I wish," I broke off, trying to keep from sobbing.

More silence. I figured Greg was trying to make sense of the news his apparently hysterical sister had just dumped in his lap.

Eventually, after he cleared his throat, my brother, his voice low, said words I had never expected to hear.

"How did this woman die? What caused it?" He paused. "Please don't tell me she fell off a roof and managed to, to …" as his voice faded, I yanked the phone away from my ear, held it out and stared at it.

Did Greg say what I was sure he had just said? My own brother? The one who saw the hell I went through after

Drew's death? I could hear him talking some more but couldn't make out the words. I stared at the phone for several pain-filled seconds. Then slowly, carefully, I pressed my thumb down to disconnect the call.

About a minute later, my phone buzzed. I was still holding it in my hand, and I saw Greg's name on the caller ID. I reached down, opened my purse, and tossed in the phone.

10

I sat by my condo's lakeside window, sipping Earl Grey tea. The clear blue sky and warmer temperature, it was almost 30 degrees out, apparently were cause for great joy, as several people were walking along the beach this Saturday morning. The thought that I should join them crossed my mind. Aunt Raelynn wouldn't be back from her vacation cruise until later that day so I couldn't get a pep talk from her, urging me to enjoy the great outdoors. Instead, I kept staring at my phone, at the notification that I had voicemail.

As I stared, the phone buzzed, startling me so much I almost dropped it. I checked the caller ID. It was Sarah. I immediately connected.

Sarah wanted to know if I could drive out to her house. "I have a lot of paperwork and can't come to the shop today but really want to help with whatever you need. Kylie told me at the wake she had some web stuff done. Can I, do you mind if I look?"

Half an hour later, Sarah was sitting at her desk in the upstairs apartment, reviewing the papers I had brought, Eliot curled up on the floor near her. While Sarah did that, I checked out the display she had put together in a pine cabinet along the far wall, a mix of antique knickknacks and old stoneware bowls. "Oh, this is so cool, you really know how to showcase things." Still wandering around, I peered out of one of the room's windows, which showed the farm property just east of the house. About a hundred yards away, some stakes were visible in the snow-covered lot. They delineated an area that looked to be about the size of a large patio.

Sarah showed up at my side, and I motioned to the stakes. "Building something?"

"Nothing exciting," she said after a moment's hesitation. "The, the house needs a new well, 'cause ours, ours was failing and Mom was having the area tested and that's one of the things I need to check into and, and there's so much to be done what with the will and all and, oh I love, I adore what Kylie did with the website." Her words were coming in a rush, and Sarah paused to catch her breath, then took my arm and steered me toward the desk.

"I want to talk to Kylie," she said, pointing to the sketch I had brought. "The art of the woman needs some tweaking, she looks a bit too young for our customer base, but that won't be hard to fix."

Sarah picked up the sketch, and we headed for the wingback chairs, Eliot deigning to join us. "I'd like her to be about 35 or 40," Sarah said.

I nodded in agreement. "Great plan. I still need to finish setting up the ordering and payment process. but the end is in sight." I hesitated, then took the plunge. "Have you heard any more about your mom's death? Have the police been in touch?"

Sarah reached out and grabbed a tissue from a box on a stand between the chairs. "Oh, Lauren, some detective guy, he kept asking me a lot of questions about my trip and what was I doing that Sunday, and did I have any hotel receipts. It was awful." Her eyes welled with tears. "All I could think was how I was sitting at the Ryman, listening to country

51

music, and to think, to think that Mom was probably there in the shed, dying, and I was enjoying myself in Nashville and happy to get away from here for a bit, and, and …"

I clasped her hand. Sarah's response brought back memories of finding Bernice's body and of my own dealings two years ago with the Florida police and then with Maccini. The onslaught of those events brought me so close to tears myself that I couldn't speak.

Sarah broke the silence. "I'll come by the shop Monday and help out, do some work with the inventory," she finally managed to say. "We both need a break from this horrible time. And we might have another funeral to attend. I hear Dennis is barely hanging on. What's happening around here?"

* * *

On the way back to Alleton, I stopped at a small roadside diner. At noon on a Saturday, it was packed with people looking happy and relaxed, talking about football playoffs and ice fishing and all the normal day-to-day things I craved hearing about, a break from the drama of deaths and suspicions that had darkened my life.

After finishing my oversized omelet, apparently the diner's specialty, I accepted the waitress's offer of more tea. Then I pulled out my phone and connected to voicemail. I figured it would be easier to listen to my brother's message surrounded by a roomful of people, that it would keep me from either breaking down or throwing the phone across the room.

"Hey Sis, please, I am so sorry. Stupid me. You took me by surprise. I need you to call me back, please."

A second or so of silence, then, "You've always been stubborn. I get that I hurt you, but you can't keep pushing everyone away. I know other people hurt you, and I don't blame you for leaving here, but don't do this." Another short silence. "We're family, Vic. Call me. Please."

The waitress came by with my bill, giving me a sympathetic look. She probably thought I had been stood up by a boyfriend.

I got up, paid my bill, and left the comforting confines of the restaurant. I sat in the car, heat turned up full blast. Then I pulled out of the lot and drove back to Alleton.

11

I almost drove to the condo, but the thought of all the inventory still needing to be unpacked, priced, and shelved weighed on my mind. Bathing Beauty was not where I wanted to be on a cold Saturday afternoon, seeing people walking to the nearby Italian restaurant for a nice meal while I slogged through a seemingly endless supply of creams and potions and elixirs, feeling left out of life's better moments.

Still, it was one of life's better moments when I got to the store and discovered D.J. already there, looking handsome as always in jeans and a dark blue crewneck sweater. He'd opened almost all the boxes and had stacks of product waiting for me to point out their proper placement. When I walked in, he looked up and grinned.

"Dad's still hanging in there," he said, "so I thought I'd come by, make some money today." He stared at me in surprise when I burst into tears.

"This was supposed to be good news," he said.

"Oh, D.J, you've given me two pieces of good news this morning," I told him, "your dad's still fighting, and the shop might actually open in February. How could I not cry?"

"Women," he said, slapping his face lightly. "I don't understand them at all."

"Oh, ask Freud," I said, "he'll tell you nobody does."

As I sat at the computer, entering prices, D.J. spent the

next couple hours putting products away. Bathing Beauty was starting to look like an actual store instead of an empty box.

Finally, we took a break, and I showed off my new coffeemaker. "This was Kylie's doing," I said as I made coffee for D.J. and tea for me. "That girl can get what you need."

D.J. took a sip, then pursed his lips. "We had a long talk at the hospital yesterday," he finally said. "And we both agree there's nothing there to save. She was pretty teary about it all, even though it was mostly her idea." He sighed. "Again, I just don't understand women."

"You're young," I said, sounding like his mother even though I was only seven years older than him. "You have plenty of time to learn that you won't ever understand women."

Our laughter was interrupted by a knock on the door, and I heard Frank's voice as he yelled into the shop. "We know you're in there, you can't hide. Let us in."

Frank and Justin came in, and Justin checked the store out and let out a whistle. "Looking good," he said. "and I love the new lighting. I kept telling Bernice the store was too dark, made everything look dingy."

"Oh, Sarah gets credit for the new lighting, she oversaw the installation right after Christmas, and D.J. gets credit for getting things stocked. Who needs me?"

Frank held up a hand. "We do! In fact, that's why we're here. Want to join us for an Italian dinner? We have things to discuss. D.J., you can come, too."

D.J. waved and put on his coat. "Thanks, but nope. Need to get back to the hospital. Mom's going stir crazy sitting in the waiting room. I think a quick burger and beer break would help both of us."

* * *

Antonelli's normally would be jammed on a Saturday night, but since the tourist trade had slowed for the winter, the three of us had no problem getting a table. We hungrily grabbed the garlic toast when it appeared and decided that sharing a bottle of Chianti, maybe two, was just what we all needed.

"What's up, guys?" I asked the Waves End owners. The pair had yet to reveal what it was they needed me for, enjoying being mysterious.

"First," Frank said, "we're canceling tomorrow night's January Doldrums gathering. The wake was enough excitement for a while. But more important, we have a job for you." Frank tilted his wine glass at me. "And you can't say no."

"Hmmm, I feel a bit like you're playing the Godfather, with an offer I can't refuse. Go ahead, hit me with your best shot."

"Here's the deal. We want your blood. Well, we don't, but Kylie does. We're just her PR folks." Frank, dressed relatively sedately for him in a light gray Fair Isle sweater, gave me one of his devilish grins.

Justin pushed up his hipster glasses. "Frank, you always skip the important details. Kylie doesn't want your blood, Lauren, she just wants to know what your HLA type is."

They continued to give me Cheshire Cat smiles. "You don't have a clue what we're talking about, do you?" Frank asked.

As we picked at the antipasto, Frank told me about Kylie's plan to start a bone marrow registration drive. After a lot of tests, her niece, Evie, had been diagnosed with aplastic anemia and needed a bone marrow donor.

"I don't know what that means, but it sounds scary. Is

Evie's life in danger?" I pictured the sweet, shy toddler, now understanding why she didn't bounce around like most four-year-olds.

"I'm afraid it might be. The doctors can treat her for a while, but a bone marrow transplant is her only real chance at surviving the disease," Justin said. The three of us sat quietly for a moment, not wanting to believe the tragic possibility.

"It's all so damned unfair," Frank finally said. "And since she's adopted, she doesn't have any blood relatives available who might be a donor match. Kylie came up with the idea to ask Alleton merchants to join the registry. She needs big numbers because a match will be hard to find, and this is not the most diverse town. That's why we all need to get involved."

Justin reached over and tapped my hand. "Kylie is quite the organizer, and she set up official committees. Frank and I oversee recruiting donors. And we are recruiting you."

"A little fresh blood, you might say," said Frank, never one to let a joke pass by. Justin gave a see-what-I-put-up-with sigh, then smiled.

"You know I'll do whatever needs to be done," I said, "but I have a question. What's the deal with Evie and her parents? I know Kylie doesn't seem to mind all the babysitting, but where are Evie's mom and dad in all this?"

The waitress came by with our entrees, glazed salmon for me, baked mostaccioli for Justin, and some heavenly smelling bouillabaisse for Frank, which put a temporary stop to our conversation. Eventually Frank picked up the thread.

"Nobody likes to talk about it, because it might be unfair to Evie's parents to point a finger — and you know how much I hate to gossip," he winked at me, and I saw Justin roll his eyes, "but Evie turned out to be more difficult than Christie and Tom were expecting. Not saying they don't love the little tyke, but she needs such close supervision and her medical bills are so outrageous that they work extra to cover the expense. Christie counts on her sister to help out.

"Ahhh, enough with this downer talk. We're going to get Evie a bone marrow match and she will be healthy, and Tom and Christie won't be under such stress, and Kylie can focus more on her business, and we can all live happily ever after."

He lifted his glass of Chianti in a toast, and we all clinked glasses.

I didn't know about happily ever after for all of us, but at that moment I was feeling happy. Not for what Evie was facing, of course. But for the first time since I'd moved to Alleton in October, interrupted by a short trip back to Tampa in December, a visit I didn't want to end, I felt like I was starting to belong here. Bernice's death, Maccini's suspicions, Sarah's secrecy, Kylie's questioning, and my brother's unanswered message all faded away.

I lifted my wine glass for a second toast.

"Here's to Kylie," I said, "and her bloody good idea."

12

When Aunt Raelynn's face appeared on my computer screen in response to my Sunday morning video call, my world suddenly became a better place.

"How was the cruise, Ms. Minnie?" I managed to ask through my laughter.

My aunt sported a pair of Mouse ears and a Minnie Mouse T-shirt. "That's Princess Minnie to you," she said. "And you know I adore Disney dazzle. The girls loved it, and even Garrett was happy because the food was good 'n' plenty. But all good things must come to an end. Now I have to get back to blessed reality and do laundry."

Aunt Raelynn and her husband, Garrett, were the grandparents of six-year-old twin girls. The cruise had been a Christmas surprise for them, and I knew Raelynn and Garrett had scrimped and saved for months to pay for the gift. I also knew better than to offer to pitch in.

"Don't want to mix money and friendship," Aunt Raelynn once told me. "You need to love people for who they are, not what they got."

The call was a distant second to what I really needed, which was the warm presence of the woman who had watched over me while my parents worked all kinds of odd hours, keeping their realty business afloat. She saw me through my angst-ridden teenage years, convincing me that the boy who paid no attention to me just wasn't worthy of my tears, and that life was full of ups and downs for us all, but we could still sing and dance and appreciate the good stuff while working to get through the bad stuff.

Aunt Raelynn, who looked like an earth mother with her caramel brown hair tumbling to her shoulders, light brown eyes, and golden skin tones, suddenly leaned in and gave me one of her typical don't-mess-with-me stares.

"Sweetie, what's up? You've always been thin, but now you look skinny as a pea turkey and that smile needs a sprinkle of pixie dust. Talk to me. Are you too lonely? Do you need to see a grief counselor up there?"

Her concern was all it took to shatter my resolve not to throw all my problems her way. I told her about Bernice's death, about Detective Maccini's suspicions, and about Greg's slip of the tongue.

"And if it gets any colder, I'm going to turn into an ice sculpture," I finished with a dramatic flourish. Then I shook my head. "Sorry, I sound like a spoiled brat."

Aunt Raelynn reached out a hand, as if we could touch across the thousand miles that separated us. "Oh, Sweet Pea, you don't sound like a spoiled brat. You sound like someone in danger. Whoever killed Bernice might be setting you up."

I'd deliberately ignored that possibility, pretending the world was still a sane, normal place that wasn't out to destroy me more than it already had.

"Do you feel like you should come home?" Raelynn asked. "You can stay here for as long as you want."

Typical Raelynn. Not offering advice, simply presenting an option.

I looked away from the computer screen to the clouds scudding by outside. Did I want to leave, run from a new set of problems?

Finally, I turned back to the screen. "What's with you, always making me think?" I asked and got a grin from Raelynn. "No, I don't think leaving is a good plan. Bernice had a wide social circle, and the killer could be someone I don't even know."

Aunt Raelynn took off her Mouse ears. "Three things, no arguments accepted. Be very, very careful. This is serious. Second, let's keep this a secret from your mom. She would go nuts because she can't come flying to your rescue. Last, call Greg. He loves you."

I could hear the voices of the twins in the background, anxious for grandma's attention.

"Sounds like you have to go," I said. "But I promise I won't be stupid, or at least more stupid than I've already been. We both know telling Mom definitely would be stupid. All hell would break loose." I laughed. "And, yes, I'll call Greg soon."

The one thing neither one of us could promise was that we wouldn't cry as we bid each other farewell.

After I got my emotions under control, I decided it was time to do some good works. The list Frank and Justin gave me contained the names of several retailers, including merchants at the Alleton antique pavilion. I figured a few of them might be there on a Sunday, so I stuck a handful of information sheets that explained the bone marrow drive into my purse and headed out the door.

The two-story antique mall was not exactly busy, and most of the booths were not staffed by their owners. I checked out a couple booths, seeking ideas for interesting gifts, then managed to talk to five retailers. Three of them expressed an interest in the drive, although having to visit a doctor and submit to a blood draw curbed some of their enthusiasm. The other two were older than 60, past the age the registry would accept.

"Well, shoot," said a booth owner who introduced himself to me as "Gus the book guy." He was probably in his 80s, with thinning white hair and bushy eyebrows. "You get old, and you can't even give your blood away."

"Weren't you at Bernice's wake?" I asked, his well-worn face stirring a memory of that night.

"Sure was," he said, "but I left before all the excitement." Bernice was a friend of his, he told me, and wasn't that a darn shame what happened to her. I didn't tell him about my discovery of her body but did say she had run a wonderful store and I felt privileged to take it over.

"You were a darn sight lucky on that one, miss. That was a hot bidding war going on when she announced she was selling. I'm surprised she sold it to an out-of-towner. Woulda thought she'd go local. But that was Bernice, always a sharp eye on the kitty."

Keeping my tone casual, I expressed an interest in who the bidders were.

"Lemme think. A couple out-of-towners like you, a local young hopeful, probably didn't have the cash, and it seems like those toy store folks had a yearning for the place."

He scratched his stubbly chin. "That Bernice, she was a tough one. Didn't want to sell to people she didn't approve of. The big thing, and I told this straight out to Bernice, was she was being awful spiteful to that daughter of hers, not giving her a chance at the business. But Bernice just gave me her trademark evil eye and said Sarah wasn't smart with money. Course, I knew better than to ask more questions."

I didn't tell him what Natalie had said to me at the wake about Bernice's fears over Sarah wanting to sell more high-end products, certain Gus would still think Bernice was wrong to punish her daughter. The longer I knew Sarah, the more I agreed.

Gus reached out and patted my hand. "Bernice had an eye for winners, so I ain't wishing you luck. Don't need it. You'll do fine. Now that little girl, the one who needs bone marrow, she needs more than luck. You take her my prayers."

I stopped at a few other places on my list, including two bed and breakfasts. The owner of one said she couldn't arrange for a blood test because the B&B took all her time. The second couple, cleaning up after their big Sunday brunch, wanted to help. After the husband looked over the information sheet, however, he said he and his wife wouldn't be accepted by the registry for several months. Both had gotten small tattoos last fall to celebrate their fifth anniversary, and you had to wait a year or so to be eligible after getting a tattoo.

Evie, I realized after reviewing my disappointing results, needed something in addition to luck and a prayer to beat her disease. She needed a gigantic pool of people willing and able to join the registry.

13

Sarah showed up Monday morning as promised, and I was thrilled to see her. In her tailored black wool pants and blazer, she looked professional, in contrast to my thick sweatpants and sweatshirt. Sarah quickly dealt with the artist who was repainting the Bathing Beauty sign, the two of them discussing details of color and shading that made my eyes glaze over. She also redid some product shelving, explaining to me the way shoppers generally behaved.

I thought about what Gus the book guy had told me and felt again the unfairness of Bernice's decision to bypass her daughter and sell the store, even if I had profited from that choice. But Sarah's demeanor and actions showed no sign of enmity toward me.

We stopped work for a while to gobble down sandwiches we'd earlier grabbed from the diner down the street. We had just finished when someone pounded on the shop door, yelling. I ran to the door, peeked around the edge of the shade, and saw D.J. outside, fist raised to hit the door again. I yanked the door open, and he almost fell in.

He staggered, then collapsed on the floor, sobbing so hard we couldn't understand what he was trying to say.

Sarah bent down and put her arms around him, holding him close, rocking him. "Shhh, shhh, it's okay, D.J. we can help. What happened? Tell us what happened."

D.J. took a deep breath, a shudder running through his

body. "My dad," he said, "he's dead." Sarah and I looked at each other in shock, but D.J. wasn't done.

"They say he was murdered, and the cops are going through the house and the shop, they got some kind of warrant and they kicked us out," he cried. "They just came by and made us leave and my mom sent me down here and she went to the store and," he hugged Sarah so tight I thought he would break her, "and what are we going to do?"

I stood up. "Sarah, okay if I go check things out?" She nodded, still holding D.J., and I ran to get my coat.

A few people were out shopping, and the spicy aroma from Antonelli's filled the air, but my attention was on the scene in front of the Wooden Block. I could see Tami out front, her down jacket unzipped, hands shoved into pockets, while a police officer stood guard by the shop's front door. Two police cars, idling but with no sirens or lights, were parked on the street. One of them was an Alleton vehicle, the other a county cop car. Did that mean Maccini was there? I had no clue how the Michigan police agencies worked, but maybe a homicide in Alleton meant the county force was involved in the investigation.

I rushed over to Tami, who threw her arms around me. "D.J. is at Bathing Beauty with Sarah," I told her. "How are you? Do you know what's going on?"

Tami released me and stepped back, incomprehension on her face. "The hospital called in the middle of the night, said to get down there fast. D.J. and I rushed over, and when we got there, we held his hand, but he just slipped away."

She seemed on the verge of breaking down again but pulled herself together. "That was terrible, but then the cops showed up this morning, waving a warrant in my face."

She glanced at the officer by the shop door and moved away slightly so he couldn't overhear. "You know what they said? They said we had to get out of the house because they had official approval to search it and we had to come down here and open the store, so they could search it, too."

Tami pulled some papers out of her pocket and thrust them at me. "They told us the doctors think he was poisoned, and we had to wait here until they could talk to us and I don't know what the hell is going on or what they are looking for, but they wouldn't let me go back to the hospital and see Den, and," anger was starting to replace her tears, "I want to talk to the person in charge!"

Her spurt of words left me reeling. Dennis, poisoned? Bernice, overdosed with sleeping pills? And what did the police expect to find at the Tomlinsons' house and store?

Winter's chill was seeping into my bones. "Tami, why don't you come to my store? I'll get you something warm to drink, and you and D.J. can talk there."

She nodded and walked over to the officer on guard. Her fury was clear. "I'm going to the Bathing Beauty store," she snapped at him. I was glad he told her it was okay as long as she stayed there until a police officer arrived. I feared she might have slugged him if he had disagreed with her.

Sarah and D.J. were sitting on the office chairs when Tami and I arrived. D.J. jumped up and hugged his mom. They both looked on the verge of collapse.

Tami sat on a counter near Sarah and D.J., and I played hostess. Tami took the hot chocolate I gave her as if it were a lifeline and reached over to pat D.J.'s cheek. "You okay, son?" she asked.

He gave her a lost child look. "They think someone killed Dad? Do they think we did it?"

Tami had no response. Instead, her eyes roamed the room. I knew precisely what was happening. The idea that her husband was dead was starting to sink in, and she was seeking guidance, something to help her through this new life. Never mind that she might be a suspect in his death, that hadn't hit home yet. D.J. still looked stunned, as if this all couldn't really be happening, but Tami had gotten the message, as much as she wanted to pretend it was not real.

Sarah and I quietly drank the tea I had made, me sitting near Tami on the low counter, occasionally reaching over to touch her shoulder.

We all might have stayed that way forever, D.J. frozen in disbelief, Tami trying to process what the day had meant, and Sarah and I seeking desperately for something to say or do that would comfort the grieving mother and son, but a knock on the door broke the spell.

I got up, pulled aside the front-door shade, and shuddered. Maccini and a police officer I didn't know stood outside. I reluctantly opened the door, and Maccini gave me a curt nod as he stepped inside the shop.

"Mrs. Tomlinson, D.J., sorry 'bout the delay. But I need both of you to come to the station with me. We need to go over a few things."

Any hint of a caring counselor was gone. He and the other officer, who had not been introduced but was wearing an Alleton patch, looked stern and in command.

Tami, however, had a backbone, too. She slid off the counter, lifted her chin, and pointed a finger at Maccini. "Why don't you tell me what's going on? What were you looking for at my house, at my store? And what do you need to talk to D.J. about?"

The Alleton officer moved slightly toward Tami as if he feared she might launch herself at Maccini. But Maccini shook his head at the officer and spread his hands out. "We're asking the questions, not the other way around."

"What if I don't want to go to the police station?" Tami

said, putting her hands on her hips. "Are you going to arrest me? Or D.J.? Or are you going to arrest us both?"

Maccini took a deep breath and scowled right back at Tami. "You both are material witnesses. And it would help us find out what happened to your husband if the two of you would talk to us."

I had gained a rudimentary sense of police procedures in Florida and decided it was time to step in. "Give us a minute," I told Maccini, who glared at me. I motioned Tami to the back of the store.

"I don't mind helping out," she told me, her anger apparently diffused by Maccini's suggestion that she could aid in the search for her husband's killer.

"Oh, Tami, I'm sorry to have to say this. Even though he hasn't arrested you yet, you obviously are a suspect. I suggest you talk to him, but only with an attorney. I'm not joking. Don't say a word until your attorney is with you. And tell D.J. the same thing. You need to protect yourself — and him."

She looked at the ceiling, as though seeking a divine message, but I could tell my words had connected. "Okay, I'll do that. But an attorney? Isn't that expensive?"

I took her hand, gave it a quick squeeze. "This is not the time to worry about the cost. This is the time to worry about your future."

14

After everyone left, Sarah picked up a box, put it back on the floor, sighed. I opened my laptop, glanced at the Excel file of prices, then shut it down. We each grabbed a chair.

"My mom and now Dennis, what, what does this mean? I'm getting scared, Lauren," Sarah twisted her hands together, her breathing rapid.

I lifted my shoulders, no words coming. I could hardly reassure her. All of this was scaring me, too.

"I'm going to stop by Waves End and talk to Frank and Justin," she finally said. "They need to know what's going on."

I figured Frank, with his Alleton network, probably already had heard the news, but Sarah might feel better talking to him. They'd known each other for years, and I was a relative newcomer in her life.

So far at least, she didn't seem to know that I was among those under suspicion for her mom's death, and I wasn't about to tell her.

Back at my condo, I uncorked a bottle of wine and pulled out my phone. I listened to Greg's message again. He left it three days ago, and I knew if I didn't return it soon, I might do irreparable damage to our relationship. But it was Monday night, which meant he would be at home with Carmen and little Roberto. Not the best time to call.

Taking a huge swallow of wine, some liquid courage, I

thought, "To hell with Carmen." Too bad if she didn't like the idea of me staying in touch with my own brother. I couldn't tiptoe around her feelings forever, and I needed to stay on Greg's good side. Standing by the balcony's sliding door, too nervous to sit down, I put the wine glass down and made the call.

"Vic, how nice of you to call me back. Been busy?" I grabbed on to the nearby recliner, Greg's first words, his cool voice, sent me rocking off balance. Well, what did I expect? The guy was mad, and I couldn't really blame him.

I took a deep breath. "I'm so sorry, Egg. Yes, I've been busy, and I'll tell you what's been going on up here. But it was wrong of me not to answer when you called back. You just hit me with a nasty shock. No excuse, really, big brother, but I hope you'll forgive me."

"Listen, Sis, now I'm the one who's busy, so I can't really talk. What I said about falling off a roof was wrong and hurtful, but it's hard to apologize if you won't even take my call. So maybe we're even. And I really have to go. I'll call you back in a few days. Bye."

The call was disconnected. I reached over, picked up my wine glass, and threw it against the wall. The shatter-proof glass bounced off, landed on the floor, and rolled. Now all I had to show for my fit of anger and rage, and, let me be honest, embarrassment over my childish act of ignoring Greg's call, were red stains on the wall and carpet.

15

I dragged myself out of bed, paying the price for finishing off last night's bottle of wine. Aunt Raelynn sounded in my mind, cautionary words about giving and taking, forgiving and forgetting.

Moping around wasn't doing me any good either, so I scrubbed the wall and carpet of my evening anger, dutifully did a physical workout, then headed out to check more names off the list of people to inform about the bone marrow registry. If nothing else, I could try to help Evie.

First, I drove by the Tomlinson house, my curiosity over the fate of Tami and D.J. too much to ignore. Like many of the retailers who kept the coastal town a must-visit for tourists, Tami and Dennis couldn't afford the high prices of houses in town and, like Sarah, lived a few miles from Alleton's lakeside condos and multimillion-dollar mansions.

Their two-story, shingle-sided place looked empty, and no one responded to my knock on their door. I hoped the lack of response didn't mean they were both sitting in jail. That would have been too much for me to take in.

I made my appointed rounds, stopping at more B&Bs, visiting hair salons, gas stations, restaurants. The willingness of many to give up some time and blood to help a little girl most of them had never met helped pull me out of my funk. Maybe Raelynn had it right after all, and the good can outweigh the bad.

When my list was done, the day stretched before me. Thanks to D.J. and Sarah's efforts, and despite my worries, Bathing Beauty appeared to be on track to open in little more than three weeks. A final shipment of botanical products was due in on Thursday, but the shop wasn't in need of my presence that day or the next.

Still worried about Tami and D.J., I decided to stop by Waves End, see if newshound Frank might know the score. The shop's bell jingled as I entered, and I made my usual obeisance to the metal sculpture of the angry creature, always reaching, never connecting.

"You really should buy that, you know," Justin said. Looking every inch the cutting-edge artist, with his slouchy gray sweater and carefully arranged black-and-white scarf, he'd been installing some pieces of fiber art when I came in. He walked over and traced a finger along one of the statue's outstretched hands. "It speaks to you."

He saw me glance at the price tag. "I know, it's a big investment. But maybe it's worth it to you."

Thanks to Drew's insurance, I could easily afford the piece but was not quite ready to think in terms of buying art and setting up my own household in Michigan. My lonely life was so unsettled, I couldn't even figure out what state I wanted to live in. And I knew I couldn't live with the statue. Too much rage.

"I know I know, you'll think about it," Justin said, smiling. "The words all shopkeepers hate to hear. It means the customer will walk out, never to be seen again."

"You can't get rid of me," I assured him. "Where would I get all the news? And speaking of the nosy news guy, where is he? I'm anxious to find out what happened with Tami and D.J. yesterday. Are they in jail?"

"They are not in jail, they are with that nosy news guy. He traded treating them to breakfast for an update. Sorry, don't mean to make light of the situation. We're all worried about this mess."

Justin's update was reassuring, however. He didn't know a lot because Frank hadn't reported back from his breakfast meeting, but he did know that the police had told Tami and D.J. that they were temporarily in the clear. Apparently, the police were still checking some of the items they had taken, but Tami and D.J. had been told that nothing immediately suspicious was found at their house or shop.

"They took stuff from the Tomlinsons' bathroom cabinets and other things from the kitchen," Justin told me. "Tami said they were cagey about what exactly they wanted, and they haven't told her yet what killed Dennis."

"Still, she can have the funeral soon. I guess they already got all the evidence they needed."

We looked at each other, that gruesome thought casting a pall on the conversation. Then Justin brightened.

"Did you hear? An anonymous donor paid to have a bloodmobile park in the emergency clinic lot tomorrow. People can show up, give a blood sample, and it will be sent to a nearby facility to be tested right away and see if anyone is a good match to donate bone marrow to Evie. Promising news, right? Kylie is so excited. The word is going out by social media.

"Kylie doesn't know who funded it and no one is letting on, but it is a wonderful gift."

"That sounds like fun, like a vampire party," I said, glad for some happier news. "I'll be sure to stop by. Kylie is amazing, and I hope this all works out. If Evie couldn't get the help she needs, it would just kill Kylie ..." my bad choice of words stopped me.

73

"I know," Justin said, "we're all tiptoeing around the fact of these two deaths. Even Frank isn't making stupid jokes like his usual self."

I hesitated, then decided to go ahead and ask what was probably on everyone's mind. "Does anyone really think either Tami or D.J. could have killed Dennis? I know he was difficult, but I can't wrap my brain around the idea."

"Guy was always a jerk to Tami," Justin said, "but, hell, if she killed him it wouldn't be by poison. He'd say something at the wrong time and she'd just pick up something heavy and bash his stupid brains in."

He stopped, looking a bit shocked at his own words.

"I think you're right," I said. "If someone were going to poison Dennis, the most likely suspect would be D.J. Chemistry is his thing."

It was my turn to be appalled by my words. "Forget I said that. It's not fair to talk about people like this when they're not here to defend themselves." My own experience should have kept me from saying such terrible things about a person I liked.

Justin, however, had moved on to other suspects. "What about Bernice? If someone said Sarah was arrested, no one would be shocked, 'cause the Dragon Lady wouldn't give her the shop." He straightened one of the pieces of art. "I gotta say, though, it still would feel like the police had the wrong person. Trying to picture all these people I've known all these years as murderers is more than I can swallow."

He turned and gave me an unreadable look, and I felt a chill. I was the new person in town. Was that what he was thinking? I forced myself to brush off the concern. If I thought everyone was looking at me with suspicion, just like the nasty whispers I had suffered in Florida, I wouldn't be able to get out of bed in the morning.

16

Wednesday dawned clear and crisp, and I dressed up a bit, adding a denim jacket to my black jeans. When I walked up the three steps of the bloodmobile, I almost turned around and left once I saw the interior of the traveling medical facility. The hard-edged, cold furnishings were no doubt needed to keep the place sterile, but it all took me back to childhood visits to the doctor, when those good-for-you shots hurt, and a cherry-flavored sucker couldn't ease the distress of a nurse sticking a needle in my arm.

"Don't be such a baby," I could hear Aunt Raelynn saying. "It's okay when you're a kid, but really, Vic, you are an adult. And when it's done you can treat yourself to an ice cream sundae." The thought of her laughter and hug, assuring me that everyone hated shots but ice cream offered a fine treatment for the experience, convinced me not to back out of the bloodmobile. I could even envision the mocha fudge delight that awaited.

"Lauren! So good of you to come!" Kylie, resplendent in a bright red sweater, gave me a quick hug and ushered me farther into the van. She swept her arms around the bloodmobile. "Isn't this great? The cost of all the blood tests is already paid. But no one will tell me who paid for this. It's making me crazy. I need to thank whoever it is." Her glee was almost contagious.

She pointed at a free chair. "Have a seat there, a tech will go over the paperwork with you." She glanced at her phone. "If you have time, let's grab lunch at that coffee shop down the block. Frank might join us, he's supposed to be here soon. Lots to tell you. And I am so excited!"

She turned to greet another visitor to the van while I settled uneasily into the gray chair, trying to ignore the smell of disinfectant permeating the bloodmobile.

"Hi, I'm AnnMarie," said a young woman as she walked up to the chair. She handed me a pamphlet and ran through the list of conditions that would make me ineligible to join the bone marrow registry. I already knew about all of them and had passed, lucky me, but maybe, I reminded myself, lucky Evie, too, if I were a match.

Another young woman, the phlebotomist, took AnnMarie's place. The blood stick was done in a few minutes, making me feel embarrassed at my initial hesitancy.

Kylie came by, followed by Frank, who was also wearing a red sweater. Apparently, someone forgot to tell me the proper dress code for a blood draw. "We do know how to party, don't we?" he said, then turned as AnnMarie began her list of questions.

Kylie escorted me to the van exit. "Why don't you go on to the restaurant? Frank and I can join you in a bit."

The restaurant, small and homey with its mismatched chairs, specialized in vegetarian entrées, Kylie's dietary choice, and I scanned the menu while waiting for her and Frank to arrive. When they walked in, the woman who had run through the list of questions at the bloodmobile was with them. I puzzled over why she looked familiar.

"I hope it's okay if I join you, Kylie thought I might be able to answer some questions she had. And she thought the two of you might like to hear, too" the young woman said as she took a seat. Then she smiled at me. "I'm guessing you don't know who I am. I was the medic who was there last week when you found Bernice. Probably not a night you want to remember."

Of course. The woman with the bun who had kept an eye on me, probably watching for signs of shock. Her hair was pulled into a loose ponytail today, soothing the severe look the tight bun had given her.

"Yes, of course," I said. "Detective Maccini had most of my attention that night, but I do remember you."

The waitress came by to get our orders, and when she left, Kylie was practically bouncing in her chair. "AnnMarie was one of the medics who took Dennis to the hospital Thursday night, and she has an idea of what made him collapse and eventually killed him."

Frank looked intrigued but AnnMarie looked hesitant, and I saw Kylie give her an imploring look. "I'm only doing this because you're my friend," she told Kylie, then she looked at Frank and me. "You have to promise me you won't ever tell anyone you got this from me." After all of us nodded, AnnMarie glanced around the restaurant, checking for eavesdroppers, but our section was relatively empty, yet another sign of the slower current of Alleton life in winter.

"Okay, when we brought Dennis in, he was close to cardiac arrest. He had an irregular heartbeat. And I had to hang around and write up a report, so I heard the doctors talking about how his wife had told them Dennis was on diuretics for high blood pressure. They wondered if maybe he had ingested too much potassium."

The only thing I knew about potassium was that it was in bananas, and Kylie looked just as clueless as me, but Frank tilted his head. "Doesn't that have something to do with kidney disease? I know my uncle must keep track of it. Has to eat more of it or can't eat too much of it, not sure which."

"Dennis didn't have kidney disease, far as I know," AnnMarie said. She answered our puzzled looks with a grimace. "Let me put it this way. I'm sure Dennis had been warned about the dangers of too much potassium, so he wouldn't have knowingly consumed too much of anything like bananas or some fruit juices. A major overdose might kill him."

"Potassium can kill people?" I said. "Unbelievable."

"But he didn't die last Thursday," Frank pointed out. "He was in the hospital and they told Tami he was getting better and then they call early Monday and say he's dying. I don't understand."

"It's tricky," AnnMarie said. "But if his heart was already weakened, it might finally have given out. Or maybe the doctors didn't figure out until too late what the problem was. I might be able to find out on my next run to the hospital, but right now I don't know what happened."

"Or maybe," Frank said, "that's what the cops were hunting for when they searched Tami's house and store. Maybe they thought Tami or D.J. somehow deliberately gave him potassium."

"Oh, come on," Kylie said. "What, they were looking for bananas?"

17

My visits seeking volunteers for the bone marrow drive over the past few days revealed that robust tourists were continuing their winter wonderland activities in the area, snowshoeing or cross-country skiing at the nearby state park or hiking along the beach. Other visitors contented themselves with less rigorous activities, sampling what the area's wineries and breweries had to offer, dining at their favorite farm-to-table restaurants, treating themselves to a massage, or enjoying a romantic getaway at one of the many B&Bs.

Those who decided to do some shopping were normally a welcome sight to the Alleton merchants who remained open in January, but on this Thursday those customers had no idea that all hell had broken loose in the quaint coastal village.

The police department's official finding that Dennis was the victim of a homicide made everyone edgy. A few shopkeepers told me they were wary of the people coming through their doors, wondering if the customer could be a mad serial killer. Most of the retailers, however, thought the evil might be closer to home. They were the ones who shut their doors an hour ahead of their posted closing time, scurrying to their cars before the early winter darkness descended on the back alleyways.

Kylie had invited Frank, Justin, and me to her place for

breakfast on Thursday so she could update the list of those who had been contacted about the need for a bone marrow donor and give us all a few more names. Frank and Justin had their part-time salesclerk cover their art gallery, so both could attend.

"I have some major news," Kylie said when she called earlier that morning to remind me of the meeting. "You are not going to believe this." She wouldn't divulge the news, however, no matter how hard I pressed.

I'd never been to Kylie's place before. The small cottage was on the same lot as her sister and brother-in-law's house. Christie and Tom owned a stunning mansion that sat at the end of a curvy driveway. Large windows overlooked the front yard, and the two-story home shouted architectural elegance and a high yearly income. That made sense because Christie and Tom worked for a major financial firm, both probably putting in long hours.

If Christie and Tom's house was impressive on a grand scale, Kylie's cottage had me drooling with envy. As I walked up the gravel path and through a small wooded area, I considered how different it was from Sarah's situation. Sarah had her own upstairs area in her mother's house, and she had made it her own, but she still had to use the downstairs kitchen and the privacy factor was nil. Kylie, on the other hand, had a separate house with a charming river view, and guests could enter the way I had, walking around Tom and Christie's abode, or take a smaller, separate driveway that led to the side of her cottage. The woods effectively hid her house from any prying eyes. And Kylie could take the path to Christie and Tom's place, where a side door allowed her easy entry.

I stumbled when I heard Kylie shout, "Come on in," my attention more on the view than the door to her cottage.

Once inside, I gave Kylie my coat and waved at Evie, who was standing nearby, holding a pet robotic talking hamster. She gave me one of her shy smiles. As I now understood after talking to Frank and Justin, Kylie had been pressed into service again to watch over her niece while Evie's parents were at work. A day care center wouldn't accept Evie, Kylie had told me once, because she needed special foods and close supervision, so she didn't overwork her frail body. I had never once heard Kylie complain about it, even though I knew it cut into her own work.

If Sarah had gone with a country look to suit the farmhouse, Kylie went with vintage midcentury furniture, the same era as the clothes she favored. Today she was bedecked in a pink and white striped 1940s apron over a plain white T-shirt and black leggings. She handed me a Bloody Mary, and I stirred the colorful concoction, which matched the splashes of red she had used as an accent color, with a celery stick. It was only 9 a.m., to my mind a bit early for a drink, but given the bad news that had cast a pall over the previous week I was happy to enter the festive scene Kylie seemed determined to provide. Like the rest of us, she was probably ready to move from the disheartening time, at least for one morning.

Frank stood up from a retro pink and red chair and clinked his glass with mine. "Major jealous of that apron," he said in greeting, waving in Kylie's direction. "I am sooo boring today." His cream-colored wool fisherman's sweater looked good on him, and I told him so.

"Enough with the fashion commentary," said Justin, looking cool as always in his black-and-white striped shirt, black scarf and skinny jeans. "We have mysterious doings. Frank and I have been here for 10 minutes and can't get Kylie to tell us the big news."

"Big news," said Evie, who was standing by my side, and her robo-hamster immediately echoed, "Big news."

Evie tugged on my jeans and pointed at a small circular track set up nearby. When she set her robotic toy on the track, it ran down one side then hopped onto a wheel and began running, getting his "exercise."

"That's good, Evie," Kylie told her. "But I must run a meeting now, so why don't you give your buddy a nap and color at your desk?" Evie nodded and toddled to a child-sized desk a few feet from the main area's conversation grouping.

"That's one happy kid," Frank observed. "And what would make this kid happy is a bite of your spinach quiche." He treated himself to a slice of the quiche and grabbed a seat at a mid-century Lucite and glass table.

Kylie, Justin, and I also served ourselves a portion of the quiche and joined Frank at the table, while Evie munched on a celery stick and continued coloring.

"Out with it," Justin said, tapping Kylie's hand with the handle of his fork. "Frank told me about your meeting with AnnMarie, now I'm thinking you have an update. Spill!"

"I called this meeting to talk about the bone marrow drive," Kylie said, trying to sound put-upon. "And I wish I had more news about that. Sadly, no match for Evie yet, and whoever funded the bloodmobile is keeping quiet. But if you must, I'll skip updates on that important topic and proceed to what you seem to find more pressing than Evie and her concerns."

Justin and Frank both groaned, and I leaned over and did my best impression of a petulant child. "You're not the boss of us," I said, sticking out my lower lip.

Kylie laughed. "Okay, guess I can't keep you waiting any longer. But first," her tone turned serious, "when she called last night, AnnMarie made me promise to swear you all to secrecy again. I'm not sure that's necessary. The word is all over the hospital, she told me, and no one could pin the leak on her. None of you will squeal on her, right?"

The three of us nodded solemnly, as if we were adolescents, swearing not to tell which one of us had filched their dad's beer.

"Good," Kylie said, "now here's the bit that will blow your minds. Like AnnMarie told us at lunch, Dennis did die of an overdose of potassium."

"You're about to go all scientific on us, aren't you?" Frank said. "I did my best but don't think I did a good job explaining all this to Justin."

"I'll keep that part simple," Kylie promised, "and even so, that's not the part that will blow you away. AnnMarie said the doctors found a major amount of potassium in Dennis's body, which is what made him collapse at the wake. And it's the reason they couldn't save him. His heart was just too weak.

"But here," and Kylie looked slowly at each of us, deliberately building the suspense, "is the kicker." We all leaned in. "Dennis drove straight from his usual monthly blood test to the wake. Results of that test were normal, no excess potassium present. Which means he had to get that extra potassium at the gathering."

She ended her report with a flourish. "And that means everyone who was there is a suspect."

She looked at each of us, and it seemed as if she might be expecting applause. The three of us could only stare. Frank was the first one to recover. "You can't be serious," he said.

Justin narrowed his eyes. "Are we all going to need lawyers? Does this mean the police are going to inspect our shop and apartment, like they did Tami's place?" He shot an

83

unreadable look at Kylie, who simply shrugged her shoulders. "I don't like this at all. What the hell is happening in our beautiful town?"

"I know what's happening," Frank said, running a hand over his bald head, "One of our friends is killing people."

Unnoticed by us, Evie had walked up to the table, the robotic hamster cradled in her arms. "Killing people," she said. "Killing people," the robo-hamster repeated.

-

18

We each left Kylie's with updated lists of people to contact for the bone marrow drive. After the shock of her announcement, she switched to the reason she had called the meeting in the first place. I had more B&B owners on my list, as well as a few shop owners who hadn't been available during my first round of visits.

As I drove from one bed and breakfast to another, almost always accepting an invitation to share a cup of coffee or tea and partake of one of the establishment's signature goodies, from molasses brownies to lemon squares to spiced apple cake, my sugar high was counterbalanced by my mental low.

The final stop on my list was the boutique owned by Natalie, the officious woman who certainly would provide an element of sour. She remembered me from our meeting at Bernice's wake and agreed to listen to my bone marrow pitch since the shop was devoid of customers.

"I would love to help," she said when I was done talking, twisting one of her enormous rings, avoiding looking me in the eye. "But I can't. My health just won't permit it."

I felt like slapping myself. I'd shown her the list of those who would not be eligible to serve as donors, not thinking beforehand that she was probably in her early sixties, too old to donate.

"I know you want to," I said, "but you are absolutely

right to say no. It can be a dangerous procedure, and I'd hate to see you put yourself at risk."

Natalie accepted my gracious response, then reached over and grabbed my hand. From our conversation at the wake, I assumed she was about to impart a great piece of wisdom mixed with gossip.

"I do want to say," she said, and who was I to stop her, "that when I heard through the grapevine that Dennis was poisoned to death, it has made me think about the people in our midst."

That makes two of us, I silently agreed.

"And I do believe we need to keep our eyes on that son of his. He does something with chemistry, right? Tami is so proud of him, but it will be a long time before I'd be comfortable eating anything either one of them might bring to a potluck."

* * *

Mental exhaustion was hitting me, but after my talk with Natalie, I forced myself to stop at Bathing Beauty, where Sarah was shelving the last of the shop's inventory.

"Join me for a break," she said, pulling out a coffee cup and selecting cider from the K-cup box.

Sarah had begun interviewing applicants to work a few hours a week at Bathing Beauty. I had asked her to sort through the ones who had answered our online employment ad, counting on her expertise to weed out those she found unsuitable, and told her the final choice would be a joint decision. I obviously held all the power, but she held the knowledge, and I wanted to keep her feeling wanted and needed.

"Great idea," I said, "and grab a cider for me, too. I'm about to have a caffeine and sugar collapse after my B&B visits." I didn't share Kylie's news about Dennis. The word that all of us at the wake were under suspicion would reach her soon enough, and I did not want to be the bearer of the news.

She had her own news to share.

We sat on the office chairs, and Sarah handed me some print-outs. "I have two possible employees for you to check," she said. "Cassandra and Tiffany. They can come by whenever you want next week for a second interview. But, but there's a problem with Cassandra. She works at Waves End and, and said she wanted to get out of the art gallery. The customers always wanted to talk to one of the owners, and she was generally bored."

I peered at the print-out. "She looks good," I said. "But will Frank and Justin think we're stealing their employee?"

Sarah set her cup down, then looked around as if someone were hiding in the store and might be able to hear what she was saying. "That's not the problem," she whispered, and I had to lean in close to hear. "Cassandra thinks one of the guys went through her purse, her bag, last time she was working and took a couple of her pain pills, some kind of opiate she got after major dental surgery. She didn't have an exact count, but, but before her second refill, she came up short."

Great. Frank, one of the few people in town I felt had become a real friend, might be a pill thief. Probably an opioid addict. And if the thief turned out to be Justin, that would cause my pal Frank a great deal of anguish.

I closed my eyes, wishing away the pain Sarah's news had brought.

"What should we do?" she asked, her voice still quiet.

"First," I said, hoping I sounded more confident than I felt, "set up a time for the two finalists to come in for another interview right away. We need to make the hire soon.

"Second, if we hire Cassandra, we'll tell Frank and Justin that we won't have her start until they have a replacement. Or we'd be happy to share her until that happens. My impression is that job-hopping happens a lot around here, so they might forgive us.

"Most important, we can keep her secret. It's up to her whether she tells Frank and Justin her concerns."

Sarah didn't look any happier but nodded in agreement. "That will work, I guess. I just, I just, I hate keeping secrets."

I glanced down at my cup of cider, not wanting Sarah to see my skeptical look. That seemed to be the way things were going in this beautiful little town, I thought. Secrets and denials all around.

To put a disturbing end to a disastrous day, Detective Maccini called shortly after I arrived back at the condo. "Bring a lawyer if you want," he said, "but we need to talk tomorrow."

19

No time is a good time to visit a police officer who suspects you of murder, but I was fairly certain Maccini just wanted information about the wake. I arrived at the county police headquarters at 10 a.m. and was greeted with its ubiquitous smell of burned coffee and the irritating sound of radio static. Detective Maccini, in his standard police blues, smiled when I walked in the door. Nice to know I was wanted.

The windowless conference room held its usual charm, and the two of us took seats facing each other across the steel table. Maccini didn't offer me coffee, which I hoped meant it would be a short session.

"We're checking in with a lot of people who were at Bernice's wake," he told me. "We pinpointed the fact that that's where Dennis's poisoning took place. Have you heard about that?"

Not wanting to get AnnMarie in trouble, I gave him a noncommittal shrug.

"We've been making the official finding public, in hopes someone may have noticed something," he said. "We found that Dennis went to the wake with normal potassium levels, proved by a blood test he had just before the event. At some point during the wake, he ingested a massive amount of potassium, probably a liquid supplement added to whatever he was drinking. That's what caused his collapse. Huh.

"Sadly, even with emergency care, his heart couldn't recover, and he died three days later. The doctors said that is not unheard of."

None of that was new to me, but I nodded at the appropriate places.

"We need you to put together a short statement of what you saw at the wake, who was there, that type of thing. And, now that you know what we are looking for, if you saw any behavior that seemed strange or out of the ordinary."

Maccini slid a notebook and pen across the table. "Go ahead and write that up for me. A timeline of that evening. What you did, who you talked to, details like that."

The wake had been eight days ago, and my memory of it generally revolved around Dennis's collapse. But I told Maccini I would do my best, and he gave me his counselor smile and said to do what I could. "Poke your head out and wave when you're done," he said, "and the watch commander will come and get me."

He walked out the door. Strange, I thought, he still didn't offer me any coffee.

My attempt at re-creating my experience at Bernice's wake took more than 30 minutes, and I didn't think it would be much help. I wrote that I arrived at the wake around 6:30 p.m. and talked to Frank and Tami and Sarah and a lot of other people but couldn't remember the details. I had a couple glasses of Frank's orange drink, nibbled at a mushroom dish and Swedish meatballs and spinach cheese squares, and had a couple bites of a chocolate dessert. I did recall Sarah's thank-you talk to the guests, and said I thought she was the first to leave. And I had not seen anyone walk up to Dennis and add something to his drink.

I was more specific about the events surrounding Dennis's collapse but didn't think that would help. At that point, the evil deed had been done.

I stood up, stretched, then went to the door and waved at the officer sitting at a desk outside. He got up and took my papers. "Thank you. I'll give these to Detective Maccini. He'll be in shortly."

This was taking longer than I had envisioned, but Sarah had said she'd be working at the store, so I wasn't overly worried about the time. I settled back into the unfriendly plastic chair, checking my phone for any messages while I waited for Maccini.

A few minutes later, he walked in, two Styrofoam cups in hand. I sighed. That could only mean we were in for a longer discussion.

He placed a cup on either side of the table and moved around to sit across from me. I picked up my cup, even bad coffee was welcome if I had to get through another talk with him, and took a sip. The taste surprised me. Maccini had brought me a cup of hot tea.

I looked up and saw him grin. "You suggested I should be a better investigator, that I should know that you preferred tea to coffee. You were right." He paused, as though building suspense. "So as a good investigator, I took your advice to the next level. And I did a little more investigating about you. Wow. You've been keeping a lot of secrets, haven't you?"

The counselor's voice was long gone. I glanced down at the ugly linoleum floor, wishing it would magically open and swallow me up.

20

Maccini pointed a finger at me. "I have a question for you, Lauren Andrews. Or should I call you Victoria Lauren Kittner? Or maybe just Victoria Kittner, widow of Andrew Kittner, known as Drew?"

He settled back into his chair, his gaze never leaving me.

I closed my eyes and recalled how much work it took to do a legal name change. Gathering extensive information on my life, from former addresses to education to job history, blah, blah, blah, passing a criminal background check, visiting a notary, paying almost $300 for the privilege and attending a final hearing, Aunt Raelynn offering her love and support during the long, painful process.

Maccini cleared his throat, bringing my attention back to the present. "Why'd you change your name? And why didn't you tell me about this before?"

What could I say? Would he understand my need for a fresh start, my desire to escape the suspicion swirling around me, my wish to leave behind a name sullied by those determined to find me at fault for the death of my darling Drew?

Probably not. And I had no real answer for why I had not told him of the name change when he interviewed me following Bernice's death. But hiding my previous identity had become so ingrained in me over the past few months that telling him had not entered my mind.

"Not saying? How about this one? You were questioned by Tampa police about the so-called 'accidental' death of Drew Kittner. And the insurance company took a close look, too, given that Mr. Kittner had a policy worth five million bucks, payable to you, whether his death was accidental, terrorist activity, suicide, old age or homicide. Of course, they wouldn't pay if you were the killer."

I remained silent.

He let out a long sigh. "You get my interest? You were never charged in the death of your husband, and the insurance company did fork over that five mil, but then you move from sunny Florida to the wonderful climate of Michigan. Within two months of your move, two people you are closely associated with are murdered. Huh.

"Well, Lauren or Victoria, can you help me out here?"

His damning recitation sent me back to Tampa, back to another windowless room with a police detective asking me again and again for details about the afternoon Drew died. It wasn't difficult to tell the same story repeatedly, despite the officer's continuous attempts to trip me up. And I couldn't stop crying.

The insurance company interview was no better. The agency had to pay the death benefits to the beneficiary on the policy Drew had taken out five years earlier. Originally, he had chosen his sister, Carmen, as the recipient, but he switched it to me after we were married. The company vice president, with his expensive suit and patronizing attitude, told me with a steely-eyed look that they would not pay if I were responsible for Drew's death. I cried during that interview, too, my sense of loss so profound that I could barely breathe.

Maccini rapped on the table, the noise pulling me from my pensive withdrawal. "Okay," he said, "got more questions I'm sure you won't answer. What attracted you to Alleton? Did you see an opportunity to, oh, I don't know, double or triple your insurance gain, taking advantage of the sale prices for some of the shops here whose owners were done in by the recession? So maybe it was simply a sound business decision.

"And doing my due diligence as an investigator," the sarcasm was heavy in his voice, "I did talk to your business lawyer, and he seemed to think that's all there was to it. You saw a good opportunity and grabbed it."

He took a deep breath. "Or I could buy something else entirely."

I was shaken by the undercurrent of menace in his voice, unsure of where he was going. "Maybe you've found a foolproof way to launder funds, drug money one of your Florida pals needs to hide. That's worth some investigating, I think."

His final statement, at least, finally unlocked my virtual catatonia. In fact, it made me laugh, although what I really felt was deep, burning anger.

"Now there's a stretch," I said. "You take a name change and a long-distance move and the purchase of a small shop and end up with a plot involving drug cartels and money laundering. Instead of being a world-class investigator, sounds like you are better suited to writing screenplays."

My body was shaking, but I didn't care. Maccini, however, met my anger with another grin.

"Thought you'd like that," he said. "I was just tryin' to shake you up. Nah, I don't believe you have ties to a drug cartel. But I am a good investigator, and I'll keep looking at the murders of Bernice Mullins and Dennis Tomlinson.

"You're not under arrest … yet. But hmmm, I can see you visiting Bernice earlier on Sunday, then returning for your 'official' visit. And you were at the wake where Dennis was poisoned.

"Did Bernice know your secret? Did she threaten to expose you? Had she told Dennis?

"Ah, Lauren Victoria, lucky for you, there are plenty of other suspects for me to sort through. Which I will. Unlucky for you, I just don't see one I like as well as you."

He stood up, signaling an end to our talk, although he had done most of the talking. I put my coat on, barely able to button it because of my shaking hands.

He reached down and picked up my cup of tea, still almost full.

"Guess you weren't all that thirsty. Huh."

21

Much as I wanted to drive back to the condo and curl up and cry, I had to show up at Bathing Beauty to interview the two young women Sarah had chosen as possible employees. I drove to Alleton faster than I wanted to, sliding a bit on the icy roads, so I wouldn't be late.

Sarah looked up, relieved, when I walked into the shop's office. A woman with blond hair dyed pink, who looked relaxed in her skinny jeans and chunky sky-blue tunic, sat across the small desk from her.

"Sorry," I said as I shrugged off my coat. "My other appointment lasted longer than I expected. You must be Tiffany." I remembered her from Bernice's wake, where she had been deep in conversation with D.J.

Tiffany turned out to be a good find on Sarah's part. She'd worked retail for a couple years but wanted better hours to match her college schedule. She was also personable and seemed to have a good sense of the shop's customer base. And she came with a recommendation from D.J.

"Such a shame what happened to his dad," she said once the formal part of the interview ended and we were just chatting. "I hope the store stays in business. I know he's been worried about paying for his classes, and if that store closes, he'll be out of luck."

Okay, she was a bit of a gossip, too, but not a mean one.

And given what D.J. had told me about his dad's insurance coverage, I was pretty sure D.J. would be able to continue his schooling, an observation I did not share.

Once Tiffany left, Sarah and I agreed we should hire her. But we'd also need another part-time employee.

"Cassandra's coming in a few minutes," Sarah said. "If you like her, we, maybe we should make her an offer right away, 'cause I think, I'm pretty sure she's applied at other stores."

"Agreed," I said. "And I also want you to ask her about the missing pills. See if she has a clue about whether it's Frank or Justin. If one of them needs help, we should know that. They are our friends."

Sarah bit her bottom lip. "I'll do it," she said, "but, but I don't know if she'll know much more."

Cassandra's red hair was natural, unlike my auburn-dyed mane, and her green eyes and fair skin spoke of Irish roots. She reminded me of a librarian, calm and poised, a good listener. She had dressed for the interview, a dark green blazer and skirt picking up the color of her eyes.

After she and Sarah greeted each other like old friends, it didn't take long for me to realize I wanted to hire her, too. When I made the offer, she readily accepted.

"Can you keep this quiet for a day until I let the guys at Waves End know?" she asked, her hands clasped together in an unconscious semblance of prayer. "Frank and Justin are going to be okay without me, but it's better if they hear the news from me."

"Of course," I said, then shot a look at Sarah, who let out a deep sigh. "I'm, I am so sorry to bring this up, Cassandra," Sarah said, "but I shared, I told Lauren about your concerns over the missing pills. We, we are worried about what that might mean. If, if one of the guys is addicted to the point of stealing, maybe we should do an intervention or something."

I got up to fix a cup of tea. Since Sarah and Cassandra were friends, I thought it might be better if I stayed in the background.

"Until my final refill on the prescription ran out, I kept the rest of my pills locked in my car," Cassandra said. "The one who's stealing probably knows I suspected something."

"Do you, do you know who it might be? Even maybe a good guess?" Sarah asked.

Cassandra squirmed in her seat. "It is just a guess, and please don't ever say I said this. But I think it might be Justin. He hurt his back several months ago, and …" she trailed off.

Sarah glanced up at me, still standing a bit apart, and nodded. We both understood Cassandra's unspoken link. And we both shared the same worry about the quiet Justin.

* * *

My big plan was for a quiet Friday night, but the idea didn't disturb me. I desperately needed to think about everything that was happening around me.

The move to Michigan meant several lonely nights for me, but I was past the bleak fog of grief that threatened to choke me in the first few months after Drew's death. A list of activities my grief counselor gave me before I left, one I shared with Aunt Raelynn so she could encourage me from the sidelines, helped keep the blues at bay. I went to movies by myself, visited the library frequently, and did more physical exercise than I'd ever done before. I also took nature walks, even though I looked like an overweight polar bear, as I piled layer upon layer to keep out the biting winter cold.

My mom, Wanda, and dad, Phil, were in Haiti, where

they had joined a humanitarian group renovating homes. Cell service was spotty, so we didn't talk much. That wasn't such a bad thing. My mom, whom Greg and I loved dearly but privately referred to as Wanda the Worrier, would have driven me crazy with her concerns.

Sometimes I looked through my wedding album and had a good cry.

Therapy was not on this evening's list but detecting was. After I slapped together a turkey sandwich, my hand hovered over the bottle of red wine sitting on the counter. I touched the cork gently then opened the refrigerator and took out a bottle of mineral water. Time to keep a clear head.

I set my meager meal on the small dining room area table and got my laptop from my desk. Time for some analytics, but not the financial kind.

Maccini's discovery of my past still had me rattled. I'd hoped to make friends in Alleton before sharing the real story of my background. If he leaked what he had discovered, my chance at being fully accepted by the tight-knit community might be impossible.

That wasn't my major worry, however. The detective's hints that he was focusing on me for two murders scared me. And I had a distinct feeling that Aunt Raelynn might be right, someone could be setting me up. A lot of people knew when I was scheduled to visit with Bernice. How easy it would have been for the killer to plan the time of Bernice's death, so I would find her body. And I knew too well that that put me front and center as a suspect.

It would be more difficult to point a finger at me for the overdosing of Dennis, or at least I hoped so. Supposedly anyone could have pulled that off, but the details of how it was done escaped me. And I wasn't familiar with Dennis's medical history.

Or was I?

I took my plate to the sink, rinsed it off, then sat on the front room's recliner, my legs crossed on the cushion in front of me. I closed my eyes and started breathing deeply, Aunt Raelynn's anxiety cure. I let various conversations play through my mind, not forcing them.

The relaxation effort had a side effect. Two hours later, curled on the recliner, I woke up to the squawk of a gull on the balcony. I stared over at the balcony slider, which gave me back my reflection. And I played through the episode my unconscious mind had recalled.

It was a Sunday evening in November, and I was attending my first Waves End gathering. Several shop owners were celebrating a successful Small Business Saturday. The Thanksgiving weekend weather had cooperated, offering sunny skies and temperatures in the 50s. I knew most of the people there, as they were the merchants that I'd introduced myself to during my October scouting trip.

Frank was wearing what I would learn was his typical party look, a funny apron over jeans and a white dress shirt. This one said: "The last time I cooked, hardly anyone got sick."

"What's in this?" Dennis said, looking suspicious as Frank held out a plate of appetizers. "'Cause it really could make me sick."

Frank listed the ingredients in what he called his trademark spinach cheese squares.

"That's not for you, Den," Tami said, waving the tray away. "Mushrooms. Too much potassium."

Two months later, I understood why I remembered that conversation. Because I was the one who had pointed a finger at Frank and said, "Looks like you need a new apron. It should say 'Killer cook.'"

And everyone there had heard me.

22

If the mourners at Bernice's funeral had been solemn and respectful, those gathered for Dennis's last rites on Saturday were nervous and full of chatter. People kept looking around, perhaps expecting to see the devil incarnate walking into the room, and even the minister caught the unease. He stumbled through a reading of Dennis's obituary, making it clear he had no personal knowledge of the man in the casket, and spouted generic praise while avoiding any hint of the facts of Dennis's death. When he asked if anyone would like to say a few words, he was met with silence.

Finally, to everyone's relief, he uttered a final prayer and ended the service with an invitation for those present to join the family at a luncheon following the trip to the cemetery.

This time, I did go to the cemetery, because I thought Tami and D.J. might need to see a few more faces of friends there. As I stood, shivering, near the open ground, Dennis's final resting place, I saw Maccini, dressed in civilian clothes, standing off to the side. He caught my glance and lifted his chin, the look of a man ready to do battle. I returned his look. We were like two kids, set to throw grimy snowballs at each other, neither one of us backing down.

He did not make an appearance at the lunch in a nearby church's basement, an event even more depressing than the funeral. The ham on white bread sandwiches and bowls of macaroni salad, green beans, and coleslaw did little to lift anyone's spirits.

Sarah, Frank, Justin, Kylie, and I sat at one of the metal folding tables. Frank, as usual, tried to get a conversation flowing but with little success. Tami, who was walking around thanking everyone for being there, eventually took a seat next to me. I gave up on my half-eaten sandwich and held her hand.

"You okay?" I asked, realizing it was a stupid question.

She gave me a wan smile. "Den would be so mad if he could see this," she said, passing her hands above the food on the table. "And he would have been right. I could have afforded better, but I decided it was time to spend money on the shop and on me and on D.J." Her face contorted as she tried to hold back tears.

"You know, he was not the bad man everyone thinks. He worked hard, and we raised a good son together. That counts for something."

None of us at the table could say a word. What would we do? Argue with her? Offer the same platitudes we'd heard at the funeral service?

D.J.'s arrival broke the uncomfortable silence. "Hey guys, thanks for coming," he said, standing behind his mother and massaging her shoulders. "Anybody need anything else?"

His attempt at being a proper host met with shaking heads, but Kylie, at least, had the presence of mind to say the appropriate thing. "We're all so sorry about this," she said. "And we know it will take a while for you and your mom to want to go out and do a lot of socializing. But you both should know you can call any of us, and we can get together and talk or eat or just be with you."

The others at the table almost applauded. Kylie had said the perfect thing. It also offered the perfect get-away line.

We all exchanged hugs and quietly left the room. Like me, I'm sure everyone was breathing a sigh of relief.

As I stood outside the coat closet, buttoning my jacket, I overheard two women talking.

"I'm not going to book club Monday," one of them said. "I'm afraid to be out at night."

"Oh, we don't have to worry," the other one responded. "You and I have family and friends who care about us." She gave a small laugh. "The killer got rid of the Dragon Lady and Dennis the Abusive Menace, people no one wanted to be around. Maybe we should thank him."

* * *

The driver in the car behind me honked, pulling me from my reverie about the conversation I had overheard. Could it be, I had been thinking, that some individual saw himself as an avenging angel and was ridding Alleton of those he deemed unworthy of life? Or perhaps the misguided person felt he was doing a favor for those who suffered from the actions of his victims.

The idea chilled me. Because if that's what was happening in the killer's mind, did that mean he had another victim in mind? Was someone else already in danger?

I waved an "I'm sorry" to the impatient driver and picked up my speed, although I was in no hurry to get anywhere. Most of the work for the Bathing Beauty's re-opening was done, and the photo shoot to complete the store's web presence, showcasing various products and giving viewers a glimpse of the store's new look, wasn't scheduled until tomorrow.

My new employees, Tiffany and Cassandra, had agreed to pose as customers for the shoot, with Sarah taking her actual role of salesclerk. Kylie had hired a woman in her late forties to represent a mature age group and arranged for

D.J. to add a male presence. I wondered if he'd show up.

I only had to bring sustenance, Kylie said, since I had balked at being the face of Bathing Beauty.

"But you want people to relate to the shop's owner," she argued when I continued to refuse to allow her to use my picture as part of the web redesign.

"I think you're wrong," I said. "The drawing of the woman for all seasons works, customers can relate to her image, put themselves in her place."

I didn't know if that was true, but the last thing I wanted to do was show my face on social media. After Drew's death and the resulting flurry of suspicions put forth by people I thought of as real-life friends, I did my best to remove all my online accounts and any photos people had tagged as me. If social media guru Kylie was unable to find me by using the picture she had taken, I knew my efforts had been successful.

Unfortunately, I knew my reaction had raised her own suspicions. She didn't push, and I didn't explain, but if she wanted to believe I was in witness protection or fleeing an unhinged stalker, I was happy to let her think that.

Someday soon I could tell her the real reason, but I was not ready to go public with it now, given the deaths of Bernice and Dennis. That's just what I needed, facing another round of nasty innuendo that cast me in the role of a vindictive murderer when I had fled my life in Florida to escape that very thing.

23

"**Now stand over there** and reach for the jar of skin cream on that higher shelf," the photographer, a man with brown hair turning gray, instructed Tiffany. "And D.J., you stand off to the side, looking patient. No, not bored. Patient!"

I arranged bagels and cream cheese on a tray and set it off to the side and grinned at the photographer's comment. Poor D.J. was having a tough time displaying interest in the elixirs around him. Still, I thought he was happy to be at the shoot.

"Mom is having brunch with her cousin," he said when he arrived at the shop, "and I needed to get away from all the reminiscing. That's not a bad thing," he added hastily, "but, ya know, sometimes you need a break from the tears."

I did know. And Sarah, Kylie, Tiffany, and I, who had all been at his dad's funeral yesterday, were offering just what D.J. seemed to crave, a return to normalcy. Cassandra and Isobel, our forty-something model, also helped keep things light.

The process of taking just the right photo seemed interminable, and I wondered what the final bill would be. At the end, when the tired models gathered for more coffee and bagels, I was happy to see what the photographer had captured.

"You like?" Kylie asked the group when we gathered round to peer at the photographer's digital preview.

"We like!" announced Sarah. The workers exchanged hugs, then began packing up to leave.

When Cassandra entered the office to get her coat, I pulled her aside.

"I have a favor to ask," I said quietly. "Can you wait a few days before telling Frank and Justin you're leaving? And can you manage to get me into their studio when they're out?"

She looked at me quizzically. "They'll both be in Lansing all day Tuesday, meeting with Michigan's arts council. I'm covering the gallery for them and they leave me all the keys, so I can easily get you upstairs. But I don't like doing that."

Cassandra started to add more but stopped when Tiffany entered the office. "I'll explain when I get there," I whispered, and turned to thank Tiffany for her modeling contribution.

"You both will get paid for this," I said, "and you'll get paid for the training session tomorrow. I have heard that Sarah can be a tough drill sergeant, but I know she's a cream puff at heart. I have to go to the printer's tomorrow, but you will be in good hands."

Sarah and I stayed at the shop when the others left, moving the out-of-season merchandise used in the photo shoot back to the basement.

"You know, Lauren," Sarah said as we looked around the store, almost ready for its grand unveiling, "this place really did need an infusion of new energy. I, I think my mom and I forgot to pay attention to our customers' changing tastes. I'm excited about this place again."

We smiled at each other. "See you at the final January Doldrums gathering tonight," she said. "We need some fun. Too many funerals."

* * *

Frank's ability to bring the fun was on full display that snowy evening. His choice of an apron, "Sassy, classy and a bit smartassy," the sound of Copland's "Hoe Down" playing in the background, and the smell of fresh cinnamon rolls brought a note of cheer. I think we all felt the absence of Tami and Dennis that night, but the gallery's co-owners had added one of their artsy friends to the mix, so the place had a different vibe.

"Welcome, welcome," Frank told the assemblage when the clock struck seven. "And please introduce yourselves to the newcomer. This is Roger, known as the Artful Dodger because he picks people's pockets with what he charges for his sketches."

The Artful Dodger, a thin, intense guy who looked like he survived on a diet of mineral water and brown rice, had some works on display in Waves End, and I complimented him on his ability to capture the nuance of an expression with just a few strokes of the pen. "Kylie told me you're doing one of Evie," I said as I tried to wipe cinnamon roll icing off my hands. "I'm anxious to see that one."

The Artful Dodger grimaced. "I'm having major problems with it. No matter how I try to capture Evie's sweetness, her shy joy, all I get is her subconscious knowledge that her life will be short."

He looked around, making sure Kylie wasn't within earshot. "Maybe that's my own subconscious at play. Either way, I can't show it to anyone yet. Frank said my latest effort would tear Kylie apart."

So much for happy talk. And his words brought to my mind the terrifying subconscious thought I had had yesterday, driving back from the funeral lunch. If the killer was still planning on adding to his list of victims, dear little

Evie might be at risk. Would a deranged mind decide he would help Christie and Tom by removing the source of their financial problems?

Sarah tapped me on the shoulder. "Don't look so glum," she said. "This is meant to be a, a happy party. Or at least as happy as we can get, with, with the specter of death hanging over the town." She waved her hands in front of her face. "Oh no, forget, pay no attention to me. And, and I'm taking off. Need to show up at the shop early tomorrow to help Cassandra and Tiffany, help them learn how to handle payments and, and tough customers."

She gave me a quick hug, and I hugged her back, feeling hypocritical. Because while she was at Bathing Beauty tomorrow, I would be sneaking into her house.

24

My decision to creep into Sarah's house was part of a plan I had arrived at the previous evening. Once again, I sat in front of my laptop, planning to stay awake this time, and made a list of people and their secrets. The irony of my being suspicious of my new-found friends did not escape me. But if Maccini was determined to arrest me for two murders, I was determined to flush out the actual culprit.

Maybe I was out of my mind. Chasing a killer could get me killed. But I was done with running. I had run from Florida, run from the police department's and insurance company's suspicions, run from my family, run from my friends, run from my agony over Drew's death, run from my very self. I did not ignore the innuendoes, I did not stand tall, I did not look people in the face, I did not appreciate those who stood by my side.

I was a coward. But no more. Lauren Andrews, the new name I had given myself to honor Drew, was not going to run again.

* * *

Late January days in Alleton offered a mix of sunny skies and gray days, raw winds and refreshing breezes, freezing temperatures and teasing warm spells. Monday brought forth Mother Nature's nasty side, and she pitched hard pellets of sleet at my car's windshield.

Same as I had done before, I pulled my car close to

Sarah's garage. I thought about trying to hide it behind the building, but tire tracks on the snowy yard would be a giveaway. Yes, a passerby could easily see my car, but I decided to risk it. I had been at Sarah's several times, and her neighbors, even the nosy ones, wouldn't see my car in her driveway as a problem.

When I unlocked the side door with the key Sarah had given me weeks ago and never thought to request back, Eliot greeted me with a friendly swipe of his paw. I leaned over and gave him the tuna treat I had stashed in my purse that morning. If you are out on a nefarious deed, it helps to have the house's cat on your side.

For all my brave self-talk, the least little noise made me jump, and the old house let out a series of creaks and groans. The kitchen and living room looked the same as it had on my last visit to Sarah, but the stairway door was open. Eliot and I headed upstairs, he probably hoping for another treat from the home invader. Sarah had left lights on throughout the house, no doubt to avoid coming home to darkness in the winter's early nights.

Her country chic living area showed no signs of change. I looked out all the windows, could still see the stakes in the ground on the eastern yard. I took several pictures of the knickknacks on the bookcase and desk, then peered at the drawers of the pine desk. Several YouTube videos had prepared me for DIY lockpicking, but despite my unsanctioned visit to Sarah's house, picking a lock was a line I wasn't willing to cross. So when the top left drawer opened at my pull, I gave Eliot a thumbs-up.

As Eliot continued his own journey of exploration, pushing his nose into my purse, I carefully removed the papers from the drawer. Just as I placed them on the desktop, the phone on the desk rang. I gasped and jumped backward, stumbling to the floor in my fright.

I lay on my side on the sisal carpet, taking deep breaths, trying to get my heart rate under control. Eliot walked over and sniffed around my face, giving me unwanted kisses. The phone rang several times, then I heard Sarah's voice, asking the caller to leave a message. An electronic voice informed Sarah that her prescription was ready for pick-up.

I breathed a sigh of relief, scratched Eliot behind his ears, and stood up again. "Keep them in the same order," I muttered to myself as I sat before the stack on the desk.

The answer to my curiosity wasn't hard to find. The first few papers were all marked with the logo and address of a company called TowerSolutions. Sarah, who constantly complained about the lack of cell service at the farmhouse, had leased space on the farm's property for a cell tower. That explained the stakes she'd previously told me were for a new well. I wasn't sure why she was so secretive and saw no real reason for her to be. The property was in her name, and she wasn't doing anything illegal. Good for her.

I flipped through the remaining stack, careful to align the papers. The remainder all involved her work as executor of her mom's estate, a thankless but necessary chore.

Opening the desk's middle drawer gave me access to the remaining drawers, and I checked all of those, too. One drawer held a ticket from Sarah's visit to the Ryman auditorium in Nashville. She had attended a concert on Sunday night. I recalled how guilty she said she had felt upon discovering that she had been enjoying herself while her mother was alone and dying.

My final find was a list of franchise opportunities available in the Nashville area. Here, finally, was the true reason for her trip, and it wasn't to attend a concert at the Ryman. Sarah had visited several businesses in central

Tennessee. Her days had been taken up with exploring business opportunities, not visiting bars and listening to country music hopefuls.

After scrolling through the places and times of her visits, I also realized I was holding her rock-solid alibi in my hands. Sarah had been too busy to sneak in a long drive back to Alleton, kill her mother, and return to Nashville. She had no doubt shared her alibi with Maccini but did not want others to know what she was doing on her trip.

And I was holding the answer to another worry Frank continually warned me about. Sarah didn't want Bathing Beauty, I finally realized. Like me in Tampa, she wanted to get the hell out of town, create a new life for herself. But she wasn't leaving me in the lurch. At this moment, she was training Tiffany and Cassandra in details of the store's operations.

I closed my eyes in shame. Sarah was not a killer, and she wasn't trying to regain control of her mother's store. She was a friend, and it was about time I started treating her like one.

Eliot bumped my leg, reminding me that I had spent way too much time in the house. I replaced all the papers and, after one last, careful look around the room, turned and left.

25

The skies were clear when I drove away, and I started to turn into the parking lot for the all-day breakfast place, then swerved back onto the road at the last minute. No sense announcing my presence on the roadway leading to Sarah's house. Instead, I stopped at the drug store, antique mall, and the printer, where I picked up the signs and papers announcing the grand re-opening of Bathing Beauty. Sweet smells emanating from the coffee shop next door called my name, and I devoured a blueberry scone as the tension caused by my trespassing drained from my body.

The quiet click of people busy on their laptops kept me company in the homey shop as I stirred honey into my tea and thought about what I had just discovered. First, Sarah had not been responsible for her mother's death. Second, Sarah had taken advantage of the quarter-acre lot her father had given to her before his death to make some money. I didn't know why that was a secret or why she had not leased the land a few years ago, and I couldn't figure out a way to ask without revealing that I had scrutinized her private papers. Third, it appeared to me that Sarah had realized her mother would never make her a full partner in Bathing Beauty and had decided to forge her own path.

Last, and the question I had been reluctant to ask before, covered my relationship with Sarah. I thought we had developed the start of a friendship or could at least be coworkers who didn't keep secrets from each other. My prying made it clear she did not trust me. And why should she? I had invaded her privacy, although I hoped she would never discover my snooping. I had not shared information about my past with her, and she must have known I was keeping something secret. Worst of all, I had been the one to discover her mother's body.

If I were Sarah, I wouldn't trust me either.

* * *

Tiffany, Cassandra, and Sarah, each dressed in casual clothes as if they were about to clean the basement, were wrapping up the training session when I arrived. I showed them the posters for the grand re-opening, less than two weeks away.

"I don't have a sense of early February crowds," I said to the threesome. "Any idea of how busy we might be?"

Sarah shrugged her shoulders. "So much depends on the forecast. Local B&Bs say their bookings are decent, considering the season. No big storms are moving, are supposed to be coming our way, but winter isn't near done with us yet."

"Maybe the free food and coupons and giveaways will help," Cassandra said. "People love free stuff. Frank and Justin always put out cookies, but half the time I was the one who ate them if it was a slow day." She leaned sideways and pinched her muffin top. "The perils of retail!"

Tiffany pointed a finger at Cassandra. "Why didn't you tell me? I would have stopped by the gallery and helped you out!"

"So how did today's session go?" I asked as I fixed myself some hot cider.

Sarah stood up and headed for the coffeemaker. "It, I think it went great," she said, then turned back and looked at her trainees. "What did you two think?"

Cassandra let out a big sigh. "Sales at Waves End are different. Most of the art sales are for bigger amounts, so I didn't have to be fast and deal with a lot of customers. I need to get some more practice at all this."

"You're good with the products," Sarah said. "I would have bought one from you. And Tiffany, you're great with the sales paperwork but need more understanding of the merchandise. I'll send some product descriptions home with you.

"All in all, it was a good day. One more session later this week and I think, I believe we can make a go of this."

Our new clerks collected their coats, and when Cassandra gave me a quick hug goodbye, I whispered, "See you tomorrow." She nodded, turned, and left.

Once they were gone, I gave Sarah a quizzical look. "Will they be ready or were you just being nice?"

"It doesn't hurt to give people a boost," she said, "but, but yeah, they'll be fine. Tiffany only has big box store check-out experience, so she, she needs to learn one-on-one customer care, but she and Cassandra are personable. That's a, it's a big help."

We looked again at the grand re-opening poster.

"Don't be upset if it's not a huge success at the start," Sarah said. "Winter's not the best time of year for what we sell. You need to hang in there. It will work out okay."

"You're a gem, Sarah," I said, and I saw her blush with gratitude while I felt a wave of shame.

26

Cassandra had just opened Waves End when I walked in the door on Tuesday. She had added a fake fur purple boa to dress up her black and white ensemble, no doubt an attempt to go with the artistic vibe of the gallery. I handed her one of the Bathing Beauty grand re-opening posters, my cover for being at the gallery.

"When they return, ask Frank and Justin if they'll post it in the window," I said. "And I know giving me access to their living area seems wrong, but if we can figure out who the culprit is, we'll be better able to address the situation. And I promise I won't get overly snoopy."

That was a lie, but Cassandra didn't have to know that. Being devious, unearthing secrets, sneaking into the homes of friends, all those actions I found repellent, made me wonder what I had become. It was not a welcome thought. But neither was being arrested for murder.

"If you find any pills in their studio, what are you going to do?" Cassandra asked, breaking into my reverie. "You can't let them know you pried."

I thought for a few seconds. "If it's true one of them has a problem, I'll have a quiet talk with Frank and Justin about behavior changes I've noticed. Don't worry. We'll both keep this day a secret."

Cassandra stared at the ring of keys in her hand, then slowly handed them over. I headed up the stairs to the gallery owners' apartment. Once inside, I went to their bedroom, an area I'd never seen before. Unlike the primary color scheme they used in the main living area, here the artists chose a more restful charcoal, white, and dark brown to go with the large chalkboard that covered the wall at the head of their bed. Much as I wanted to check out the doodles scribbled on the board, I forced myself to stick with my plan and walked over to the closet.

It was easy to figure whose side of the closet was whose. Frank's held a selection of aprons and white dress shirts, Justin's a selection of long-sleeved T-shirts in muted colors, hoodies, leather jackets and his favorite designer jeans.

The pocket of one of Frank's winter coats, one I'd seen him wear before, did yield one item of interest, a packet containing something called naloxone. I took my cell phone out of my purse and did a Google search for the product. It was, I learned, a prescription medicine for use in an opioid emergency and consisted of an auto-injection system. The auto-injector was placed against the patient's outer thigh and pressed. It released a drug intended to keep the one who had overdosed breathing until medical help arrived.

Unfortunately, I didn't know if Frank carried the emergency treatment for himself or for Justin. But it was a telling find.

I moved from the closet to a dresser and carefully went through the drawers, then checked the bathroom cabinet. No stash of hidden drugs.

Their studio was located up a small flight of stairs leading off the loft's main living quarters. A key on the ring Cassandra gave me worked, and I entered the space, not sure what I'd find there. Frank and Justin were artists, but both said they went into gallery ownership because selling their own artwork didn't offer a decent living.

If it had been a sunny day, the room's skylight and large windows would have made the surroundings bright. Even with that day's clouds, the place looked large and luminous. I walked over and browsed through a series of unframed miniatures propped against one wall. Frank's work, small paintings of scenes from nature. He had a fondness for showing mushrooms in their natural habitats, peeking out from tree roots and hiding in leaf-strewn areas. The mushrooms made me think of the death of Dennis. I traced my index finger over one of the darker scenes, where a mushroom grew from a rotting log, and the layers of oil paint felt alive with menace.

On the other hand, introvert Justin favored bursts of color with minimal backgrounds. My lack of knowledge about art meant I didn't know how to judge their work, but it was fun to see projects the gallery owners had never publicly shared.

Again, I could find nothing hidden, even though I ran my fingers over the frames stacked up around the room. My last hope was a three-door, gray metal filing cabinet in the corner. Its drawers were unlocked, I was glad to learn.

And still feeling like a shameful snoop, I paged through files labeled "wills" and "taxes" and "legal records." Two "medical" files caught my eye, one for Frank and one for Justin. I pulled them from the drawer.

Justin's file told me what I was looking for. About 10 months ago he had been given opioids for the pain of a severe back injury. The file didn't reveal the cause of the injury, but the pharmacy statements showed he had been on opioids for eight months.

The prescription apparently had ended two months ago. I guessed that Justin's reliance on the pills had not.

A peek at my phone told me I'd been in Frank and Justin's apartment for about 30 minutes. I had found what I needed. It was time to clear out.

I locked the studio door, and as I came to the bottom of the studio stairs, I heard voices and heavy footsteps. It sounded like two people were bound for the apartment. Damn. I turned the corner into the apartment's living area, glanced around, and scurried to the horseshoe-shaped bar in the corner. I ducked under the lift gate and kneeled against the interior wall of the bar.

"How long will the water be off?" I heard Cassandra ask.

"Gotta see the problem," a rough male voice answered. "Maybe not long."

The lower section of the bar consisted of two open shelves, one holding booze, the other a row of cookbooks. I peered through the liquor bottles but couldn't see the kitchen area.

"Okay, well good luck. I'll be in the gallery downstairs if you need me," Cassandra said.

The apartment grew quiet, then I heard metallic sounds, accompanied by whistling. Great. I could only hope the unseen worker was right, it would be a quick job.

To keep boredom and nerves at bay, I sat back and looked at the row of cookbooks on the shelf. Their spines faced away from me, so I took one out, looked at its front cover, then replaced it before checking out the next one. As long as the workman stayed in the kitchen, I felt relatively safe from discovery.

Frank's cookbooks, for I assumed they were his, showcased his interest in cooking concepts, along with the works of such well-known chefs as Julia Child, James Beard, and Alice Waters.

While the whistling and banging continued in the next room my attention was caught by a smaller cookbook that focused on hiding vegetables in food. I opened it to a bookmarked page featuring a recipe for Beet Brownies. Someone, Frank maybe, had scrawled "Healthy. High in potassium" on the page.

I gasped, then quickly peeked through the gap in the cookbooks, afraid the plumber had heard me. But the whistling went on. I read through the recipe and the chef's note that everyone she shared the brownies with had loved them and had no idea they held a secret ingredient.

I closed the book, slotted it back into the shelf, and leaned against the bar. I tried to picture the food available at Bernice's wake. Orange drink, appetizers, Frank's signature spinach cheese squares, a few desserts. I recalled eating something chocolate, but the event was too far in the past for me to recall the food with any certainty. And maybe the brownies were a treat for Evie. I closed my eyes, resting my head in my hands. Justin stealing drugs and Frank cooking up treats laden with potassium. Would life ever make sense again?

* * *

Cassandra was alone in the gallery when I came down from Frank and Justin's apartment after I heard the plumber leave. She breathed a sigh of relief when she saw me. "I am so sorry," she said. "I had no idea that workman was coming. Scared me silly."

"You and me both," I said, and handed her back the key ring.

"Thank goodness I had a spare set of keys," she said, then raised her eyebrows. "Did you find anything?"

Her question jolted me. My mind was on the recipe I had discovered; I'd almost forgotten about what I was looking for originally.

"You were right," I finally said, wrenching my thoughts from beet brownies. "It's Justin. But Frank knows about it.

He carries around an emergency injection treatment to be used in case of an overdose."

Cassandra clutched her boa tighter around her shoulders and shook her head. "Oh, dear, now what? And should we say something?"

"You give it some thought, and I'll do the same. We can talk about it later, include Sarah in the discussion. But I need to get out of here. I'll see you in a few days."

I walked back to Bathing Beauty, shivering in the cold air and thinking about my two days of detecting. I was not any closer to figuring out who might have killed Bernice and Dennis, but I had done a shameful job of invading my friends' privacy. Would anyone still call me a friend?

27

That afternoon Sarah had stopped in at several downtown stores, asking their proprietors if they would display our poster in a front window. I finished inputting some prices and was ready to leave when Sarah came back from her assignment.

"Success," she declared. Almost all of the shop owners said they would display our grand re-opening poster. It was a show of how the Alleton merchants helped each other out.

I glanced at the time. "What do you think about joining me at my place for pizza?" I asked. "I'll order now and swing by Sam's take-out on the way there.

Sarah's eyes lit up. "We can check the last of the invoices and relax. What, what a good idea."

I had another idea. I was going to come clean with Sarah about my background. I was not, however, going to confess about my break-in. She would see that as unforgivable. She'd be right.

* * *

Nothing like the smell of pizza to bring on hunger pangs. I popped it in the oven at the condo to keep it warm, and Sarah arrived minutes later, laptop in hand. Looking through the online invoices took about 40 minutes, and we were both more than ready for a slice when the paperwork was finished.

"Beer? Soda? Tea? Name your pleasure."

"Beer," Sarah said, and I grabbed two bottles from the fridge and ferried them to the table. She stood in the kitchen and watched as I pulled the pizza from the oven and put two slices each on the plates I'd set out. "I'll take those," she said, and carried the plates to the dining area while I grabbed the napkins.

We sat at the table, and I noticed that she waited for me to take a bite of pizza before she started on her slice. Great. Nothing like the fear of being poisoned to add spice to a gathering.

We didn't talk much for several minutes, savoring the veggie pizza and the calm of knowing we were on schedule with work. We each decided that two slices were plenty and sat, content, when we were full.

"You want another beer? Or maybe something else to drink?" I asked, postponing what I was about to reveal.

"I'm good," Sarah said, and looked at me quizzically when I motioned to the two easy chairs in the front room and said, "Why don't we sit over here, I have something to tell you."

She settled in and I sat on the edge of the other chair, leaned in and looked her in the eye. "This is hard for me, and I need to apologize in advance for what I am about to say."

"Oh, I, I knew this was coming." Sarah sat up straight, chin lifted in defiance, like a condemned man preparing to die. "And I get it. You, you don't need me around anymore." Tears filled her eyes.

I jumped up and grabbed her hand. "No, no, no. Oh, Sarah, I am so sorry if that's what you've been thinking. No, that's not it at all!"

Sarah clutched my hand and looked up at me, eyes widening in surprise. I gently disengaged my hand from hers, went back and settled in my chair again, and reached down for my purse. I pulled out a newspaper clipping.

"You're the first person I've told this to up here," I said, "and I'd prefer you keep it a secret, at least until I have a chance to tell other people myself." I handed the clipping to her, watching her face intently.

She glanced at the paper, looked up at me, then looked back down and read through the item slowly.

"Who are these people?" she asked. "And what does it have to do with, with anything? I, I don't understand."

The clipping I gave her was an obituary from the *Tampa Bay Times*, dated two years ago, for Andrew Kittner, who left behind his widow, Victoria Bannock Kittner, his parents, a sister, and numerous aunts, uncles, and cousins. It did not mention the cause of death, saying only that Andrew "Drew" Kittner had died unexpectedly. The small photo with the obit showed a man who had a firm jawline, slight bump on his nose, and close-cut dark hair.

I reached in my purse, pulled out a photograph of a bridal couple, and gave it to her. She looked closely at the picture, looked at the headshot on the obituary, and peered at the wedding photo again. "That's you," she said, "and that's the man in the obituary." A frown creased her forehead. "And your late husband's name is Drew and, and …" The connection finally clicked. She held up the obituary in her other hand, read through it again.

"You're Victoria Kittner," she said.

I nodded, unable to speak.

She looked at me, still puzzled. "And you changed your name to Lauren Andrews." I nodded again. "But why? I still don't understand." Several gulls screeched in the background, as though adding their own protest to my news.

I held out my trembling hands, and she handed me the

obituary and wedding photograph. I put the obituary clipping face down on the nearby end table and stared at the picture of Drew and me, so happy on our wedding day, then placed it over the obituary. Sarah sat quietly.

"Drew was clearing up wind damage at our house. A tree was leaning against the roof after a tropical storm." Tears were blurring my vision. I knew I couldn't continue to talk, so I reached into purse again, pulled out a folded piece of paper. The official police report. Sarah reached over, silently, and took the paper from my hands.

The officer's report detailed the facts of the accident that took the life of my dear husband. In unemotional police terminology, the trooper said he had arrived in response to a 911 call and saw a body on the ground, a woman kneeling next to it. When he checked the body of the male, he wrote, he found no pulse or signs of life. Medics soon arrived in response to the 911 call, and they began CPR, but after several minutes they ended their efforts. The trooper called for the coroner and a detective. He wrote that the death appeared to be accidental, but it needed to be investigated.

Sarah continued to read, and the memory of that day's events came to me, unwelcome. It was drizzling. Drew was outside by an extension ladder, and I told him to hold off for a minute while I ran upstairs to put on a jacket. He handed me a small, sealed envelope, which I tucked in the pocket of my cargo shorts, thinking it was one of the love notes he frequently wrote me, and he gave me a bone-crushing hug and deep kiss. "Grab my windbreaker, too," he said. "Love you, babe. Don't ever forget that."

I had been the one who had called 911. When I walked into the backyard carrying Drew's windbreaker, he was lying on the ground. I believe I screamed "No!" I knelt next to Drew and desperately tried to find signs of breathing.

Nothing. I pressed my ear to his chest. Nothing. I got up, ran inside the house to retrieve my phone, unwilling to believe what I had seen.

The official report said the subject apparently had been on the roof, reaching for a branch of the tree, and began to slip. It appeared, the report read, that the subject had grabbed a power line that ran next to the house, then his body had swung into the tree. The contact with the tree had grounded him, resulting in electrocution.

Sarah's voice interrupted my nightmare memory. "I am so so sorry," she said, and I looked over to see tears glistening on her face. We both sat there, mute, until I was able to clear my throat and talk again.

"There was a reason I changed my name," I told her. "Two days after Drew died, the day before the funeral, one of his cousins came over to visit. I thought it was a condolence call, but that's not what it was."

I stood up and walked toward the kitchen on shaky legs. "Do you want something more to drink? Coffee, tea, something stronger? Want to split another beer?"

"Sure," Sarah said, still holding the police report. She picked up the wedding picture, laid the police report gently upside down over Drew's obituary, and returned the wedding picture, face up, to the stack.

Sarah took a small sip of the glass of beer I handed her. I held my glass as if it were a lifeline. As hard as it was for me to retell the details of Drew's death, the next part of the story left me both angry and feeling lost. It was in many ways even more difficult to talk about.

As the calming sounds of a gentle breeze washed over the room, I told Sarah about the visit from Drew's cousin, Raul, a pugnacious fireplug of a guy. He had walked into the living room, looked around to see if anyone else was present, and put his hands on his hips. I stepped back a bit, frightened, sensing menace.

"I know some cops," he said, "and I heard about the official report. I ain't buying it. Drew's an electrician. He never would have fallen like he did. He was pushed."

Raul pointed a finger at me, and I took another step back. Was he going to attack me?

"I think you were up there, too, and you shoved him. I think you killed him. And I intend to tell the police that." He narrowed his beady dark eyes, turned, and stalked out the door, slamming it behind him.

"It didn't end there," I told Sarah. "Raul is a big drinker, and I think he leaked the fact to his pals that I was getting a big insurance payout. It blew up online, people leaving comments about me. Some of my in-laws, people I thought were my friends, stopped talking to me. At the funeral, a few people refused to greet me. About a week later, someone used bright red spray paint and wrote 'killer' on my car."

Sarah gasped. I ended my recitation there and took a sip of beer.

The night had turned full dark, and I saw Sarah look out the balcony slider and frown.

"I'm really, really sorry to hear that," Sarah said. "That's a terrible thing." She jumped up and aimed for the coat closet. "I'm sorry to cut this short. But I need to go, it's slippery out there and, and I don't like night driving."

Her abrupt move took me by surprise. I had hoped my big reveal would at least earn me a hug, maybe bring our friendship closer. So much for a confession, even a partial one.

Sarah donned her coat and zipped it tight. As she started to head out the door, she stopped, turned, took a deep breath and raised a hand. "You can tell me more tomorrow, maybe, perhaps we can have coffee downtown. And I, I thank you for sharing the news with me. I promise to keep it quiet until, when you let other people here know."

She paused again, closed her eyes, then gave me a look I couldn't read. "And maybe, while we're talking, you, you can tell me what you were doing in my house yesterday." She walked out the door, gently closing it behind her.

28

About 30 minutes after Sarah left, my phone buzzed. It was a call from her. I hesitated, wondering if she wanted to discuss my unauthorized visit to her house. Better, I thought, to get it over, and I answered the call.

"Lauren, you need to get down here now! The shop is on fire! Fire trucks are, are everywhere!" Her voice was coming in quick bursts. "Oh my goodness, the place is, it's burning. Please, come quick!" Her ragged breathing filled the line.

I put my hand over my heart and inhaled deeply. "Sarah, I'm on my way. Where are you? How bad is it?" I could hear sirens in the background and pictured my lovely store crumbled into an ash heap.

"Near Antonelli's. Can't, can't get any closer. I can't see how bad it is, the fire trucks are, they're blocking the entire street. Oh, Lauren, I'm afraid it's all burning down." She broke off, crying.

"Hang on, I'm leaving now. Be safe. I'll be there as soon as I can."

I put a sweatshirt on over my long-sleeved cotton shirt, threw on my coat, grabbed my purse, locked the condo's front door, and took the elevator down to the underground parking area. As I neared the car door, I slipped on a patch of ice on the concrete. My arms windmilling, I managed to grab the door handle and right myself.

"Stay calm," I told myself, "stay calm." The trip normally would take fifteen minutes but at 9 o'clock on a Tuesday night, traffic was sparse. I forced myself to drive at a somewhat legal speed, and in ten minutes I was in Alleton's downtown district. Flashing red, blue, and white lights pulsed across the sky, and I could see a black cloud even in the winter's dark and smell the bitter odor of burning wood and some sort of chemical.

I pulled into a spot a quarter of a block from Antonelli's, jumped out and rushed down the street, looking for Sarah. I spotted her Toyota sedan but no sign of her. I raced around the corner and stopped, craning to see around all the fire trucks parked on the street.

The sight of Bathing Beauty's front entrance, with no sign of fire damage, almost made me cry. I walked up to the firetruck stationed in front of the store but saw no firefighters. As I moved closer to the store, a man dressed in a yellow rubberized jacket came striding up to me.

"Miss, you'll have to stand back. Please, stay on the other side of the street."

I shook my head. "I'm the owner," I cried. "You have to let me through. I need to know what's going on. That's my shop!"

He held up a hand. "Okay, wait, don't move. I'll get the captain over here. But you need to stay right here. Oh, what's your name?"

I told him, and he walked a few feet away and lifted the walkie-talkie in his left hand to his mouth, all the while keeping his eyes on me. I heard the squawk of the walkie-talkie and saw his lips move but couldn't make out what he was saying. In early January, I'd covered the front display window of the store in brown paper so shoppers could not peer into the shop and watch the renovations taking place.

The fact that the paper was still there, all in one piece, made me relax a bit.

The yellow-jacket guy ended his conversation and motioned me forward. "The captain will be here in a minute."

I plunked my purse on the ledge of the fire truck we were standing near and looked up and down the street for Sarah. A few people were standing outside, checking out the scene. I could see that more gusts of ash were rising from the back of the shop.

An older man, also in a yellow jacket, this one creased with soot and dirt, showed up at my side. "Lauren? I'm Captain McDougall," he said. We did not shake hands, as his gloves were covered with grime. "Let's go around back, so you can see where the fire was. Sarah is there, she's been asking for you."

I followed him down the sidewalk. Most of the shops had no space between them, so we had to walk past three stores until we reached the place where two stores were separated by a gap that led to the alley running behind the block of shops. Once in the alley, I could see a smaller fire truck at the rear of Bathing Beauty. A big trash bin, knocked on its side, blocked a portion of the alley. My nose burned from the acrid smell, and bits of ash landed on my jacket.

"Careful," said Captain McDougall as I tiptoed through the soot-encrusted gravel. Finally, I saw Sarah standing a few feet down the alley. And I could see the back of the shop.

Sarah had caught sight of me and walked carefully around what appeared to be small pieces of burnt wood and bits of trash strewn around the alley. Her down jacket was covered with ash, her face was slashed with black streaks, and her hug came with an acrid smell of smoke. We stood, arms around each other's waist, and looked at the rear entrance of the store. The back wall and door were blackened by smoke, and a rear window was smashed in.

"They, the firemen won't let us inside yet," Sarah said, her voice hoarse from the fumes she had inhaled. "But it looks like, like all the fire was on the outside." We hugged each other tightly, unsure of whether to be relieved or devastated.

Captain McDougall, who had been conferring with another firefighter, came up and stood to my side. He motioned at the back door.

"The fire started in that big bin," he said, pointing at the heavy trash container I had tiptoed around earlier. "But you see those burned items on the ground?" We looked down and over at the blackened pieces of what appeared to be heavy cardboard lying on the ground around the bin. "Those were apparently stacked against the back of the store, and a secondary fire started there. That's what reached the back door of your store."

Sarah's eyes widened. "But, but we don't ever leave boxes or trash behind the store," she said.

I knew what McDougall was going to say before the words left his lips. "I'm sure you don't," he said, sounding kind. "But someone did. And they started both fires. This was arson."

"Who would, who, oh dear, who would do that?" Sarah looked around at the mess in the alleyway, the black streaks on the shop, her shoulders sagging.

"I don't know," McDougall said. "And I'll need to talk to you about this tomorrow. For now, you need to get someone from your insurance company out here right away. And as soon as we clear this, I can let you look inside."

The yellow-jacket guy I had met earlier led Sarah and me

to the chief's car, parked farther down the alley. We settled in the back, and he turned up the heat. Sarah, bless her, had a card from the shop's insurance company in her wallet, and called the emergency number. She knew the agent, and I could hear his loud voice over the phone, expressing his dismay.

"He'll be here in half an hour," Sarah said when the call ended.

The firefighter returned and handed coffee to us. "Thank you," I said. "I'm sorry, I don't know your name."

"It's Firefighter McDougall," he said. I gave him a questioning look. "Yes, we're related. Captain McDougall is my uncle. But trust me, he does not play favorites. If you look around, you'll see that many of the other firefighters have left. It is my joy and privilege to stay and do his bidding until this scene is closed."

The captain, whose ears may have been burning, which is not a good joke to make around firefighters, opened the car's back door. "It's all clear now," he said, "you can come with me and look around. Either of you have keys to the front door? It would be better if we went in that way."

We used my key, and once inside Sarah and I looked around. All the shelves were stocked, just as we had left them. The office area looked fine. As we neared the back of the store, the damage became more apparent. An open window, which Captain McDougall said had been broken by the heat of fire raging just below it, meant smoke and soot had entered that portion of the store.

My initial reaction of euphoria at the lack of major damage quickly drained. I heard Sarah softly utter a curse word. The ceiling was blackened with soot. Two rows of botanical shower wash were covered with gray ash.

And all we could smell was the pervasive stench of

smoke.

Keith Smithal, the insurance agent, arrived about half an hour later. He disappeared inside the shop, then joined us in the alley, where Sarah and I were huddling together. He looked at the small notebook in his hand and gave us the news Sarah and I had been dreading. From what he could tell, Smithal said, insurance would cover any damages, but we faced a major problem.

"That smell of smoke is probably in your drywall and insulation," he said. "In other words, the back quarter of this building will have to be replaced for you to have any chance of getting rid of the stink."

Sarah and I stayed outside, my body numb with the cold, and we moved out of the way occasionally as the younger McDougall scouted through some of the debris, while Smithal went to get some tools and boards out of his car to cover the back window. A tear frequently trickled down Sarah cheek, smearing the black soot that streaked her face. I stamped my feet and wondered if I'd ever be warm again.

"We're not competing with anyone," Sarah finally said. "So why, why would someone want to delay our opening?" She rubbed her nose with the back of her glove, smudging more dirt on her face.

"And our store wasn't the only one in danger," I said. "If the fire really had caught, it could have burned down several shops on this block."

"No, I'm pretty sure that wouldn't happen. Firewalls were, they were required for the stores way back when to keep, to make sure fires don't spread."

"That's a relief, and not even something I thought to check on when I bought this place," I said, and internally winced at my words. Would that make Sarah feel like I was rubbing it in? But she didn't react, her thoughts no doubt still on the damage the shop had sustained.

"At least we're each other's alibis," I said in a meager attempt to lighten the mood.

"Great," Sarah said. "That means they won't believe either one of us."

We looked at each other. Sarah grinned. I blame it on her. I started to laugh, then both of us were laughing so hard we were crying.

Smithal walked up, looked at us in surprise, and smiled. "Shock will do that," the insurance agent said. "But I hope it makes you feel better. And I'll contact some construction companies first thing in the morning to get the process rolling." He looked at his watch. "That's only a few hours from now. I'll try to get a couple out here for bids right away. And I'm going to walk around and take pictures of the damaged merchandise."

He hesitated, then shared the bad news. "Don't take this as gospel, but even if a company can start work right away, from my experience, I think it'll be at least a month before you can open."

Sarah and I looked at each other.

"Guess we'll have to go get all those grand re-opening signs back," Sarah said. "And, and announce a fire sale."

Smithal shook his head as Sarah and I burst into hysterical laughter again.

29

Before I fell into bed that morning, I texted Cassandra, telling her about the fire and suggesting she not give her notice at Waves End for another couple weeks, as the Bathing Beauty opening day was obviously going to be later than originally planned.

After less than six hours sleep, I dragged myself to the fire station. Sarah was already there, sitting on a hard plastic chair, her face clean now but pale. We were ushered to the office of Captain McDougall, whose trim, middle-aged body looked none the worse for wear despite his long hours of work the previous evening and that morning.

"We're a small department, so I am also the arson investigator," he said. "My report will be forwarded to the Alleton police, and they'll probably contact you soon with more questions."

When he asked where Sarah and I had been yesterday, I was careful not to look her way as we alibied each other, afraid I would start laughing again. The captain didn't remark on our statements but took careful notes. If suspicions got too intense, I figured the local police could check and find some proof of our innocence, like what time I picked up the pizza, or what cell phone towers said about my location when Sarah had called about the fire. Maybe one of my neighbors had seen Sarah arrive or noticed her car in the visitors' outside parking lot. And experience told me that the insurance company would do its own investigating.

We were no help when Captain McDougall asked us who might want to burn down the store. Enemies? Business rivals? The phrase "random killer" entered my mind, but I didn't go down that crazy street.

When we left the fire department office, Sarah suggested we return to my condo and discuss our options for a different opening date. "I also have an idea I want, I need to discuss."

She didn't elaborate, but I wondered if she would ask me about my unsanctioned visit to her house.

At the condo, coffee for her, tea for me, we sat across from each other at my dining room table. We each flipped through the photos we had taken earlier that morning of the interior of Bathing Beauty. Our insurance guy, Smithal, was true to his word and had contacted a couple of renovation firms. We were scheduled to meet with them at the shop the next day.

Sarah pointed to the photo showing the back corner of the shop, an area that would need extensive renovation work. It also was what we both thought of as an awkward space because it did not flow smoothly from the front of the shop. The office took up the other corner, and customers had to move to their left, around the office, to find the area.

Sarah opened her laptop and hit a couple of keys. She turned it to me and I saw an architectural blueprint of what appeared to be a foyer leading to a smaller room.

"This," she said, pointing to the enclosure, "would be a spray-tan booth. Customers could, they would disrobe in the outer foyer, which is enclosed, enter the smaller booth and, and be sprayed with a tanning solution. That would take only a few minutes. Once it's done, they go back into the

138

outer area, put on a moisturizing lotion and get dressed."

She looked at me, her eyes questioning. "I think it's a great service for all the winter-pale people who, who don't want to hit the beach looking like the white belly of a fish. I also think it would be a hit for all seasons, because most women these days don't wear nylons, but, but they don't want to show up with pale legs.

"I, I checked all the Alleton beauty salons, and none of them offers this service."

She leaned back, crossed her arms, and shrugged her shoulders. "What do you think? We already have to renovate that section of the store, so it would be an easy change."

"I like it," I said, my mind immediately turning to financial considerations. We would need two bids from the renovation companies, one for repair of the corner and the second for the redesign. We'd pay the difference that the insurance wouldn't cover. But it could work.

Sarah raised her clenched fists in a victory cheer. "I'm so glad," she said. "I suggested, I talked about this with my mom, but, but she was never one for moving forward."

Before any sense of celebration could overtake the room, Sarah closed her laptop, took a deep breath, and stared at me, eyes narrowed. "And perhaps, maybe now is the time for you to tell me why you were at my house Monday. A neighbor saw your car in the driveway."

"Give me a minute," I said. I got up, went into the bedroom and picked up a medium-sized box, wrapped in bright blue paper with a white bow on top. I caught sight of my face in the mirror, pale and drained, and forced a smile to my lips. Back in the living area, I set the box on the table in front of Sarah.

"Go ahead and open it," I said, "then I can explain."

She carefully removed the bow and unwrapped the paper, opened the box, and reached in to pull out the object inside. About seven inches high and five inches wide, it was swathed in tissue paper. She pulled off the tissue paper and looked at the object, then placed it on the table in front of her.

I reached across the table and dropped a penny into the small platter that was held up by a miniature cast iron pig, who was sitting on a log. I pressed down the small lever coming out of the pig's back. The pig's arms lifted the platter, and the coin dropped into the pig's open mouth with a soft clunk.

I pressed some buttons on my phone and showed Sarah the screen. The first picture was of her pine desk, the mechanical piggy bank sitting on top. I revealed the next five pictures, each a close-up of the bank.

"I know how much that bank means to you, because it was a gift from your dad," I said. "And the owner of one of the booths at the antique mall said he thought he could take a piece of this bank that he had in stock," I pointed to the one on the table, "and replace the broken section of your bank. Then yours would work. You'd have a bank that would be mostly the original one your dad gave you, with a minor tweak so the pig would take the coin."

Sarah just kept looking at the bank. "I went to your house to take the pictures of your bank," I said. "And I'm sorry if it seems like a stupid idea. Maybe you don't want a hybrid of the bank. And I was going to give it to you to celebrate the re-opening of Bathing Beauty, but you needed an explanation of why I sneaked into your house …"

Sarah touched the mechanical piggy bank and looked over at me. She blinked away tears. "That is, that is one of the most wonderful, thoughtful things anyone has ever done for me," she said. "And I, I would love it if the antiques guy could fix mine. Unlike my mom, Dad always believed change could be a good thing. He, he would think your idea is a grand one."

I brushed away my own tears. Yes, I had meant to do it as a surprise for her, and I hoped it would make her happy. But I knew those good intentions were mixed with my own agenda, and a lot of my own happiness was because I had gotten away with my illegal home invasion and had not damaged our relationship.

Although her heartfelt reaction of thanks made me feel like a swine rolling in filth, I did not regret my actions.

30

"I love my grandbabies," Aunt Raelynn said when I called her after Sarah left, "but sometimes they can be sour pickles." She puckered her face at the screen, then grinned.

I made the video call to update her on the latest disturbing events, but before launching into my tale of disaster, I was anxious to hear about a life where normalcy reigned. Raelynn didn't disappoint, regaling me with her day's domestic crisis.

"One of the twins' friends just got a cat, and Taralynn and Darlene think life would be perfect if I adopted one. I explained that a cat would not be perfect for their grandpa's allergies, and their faces just crumbled. Tara yelled 'It's not fair!' and stomped outside, where she threw stones at the playhouse. Dar sulked on the sofa, muttering about how she never gets what she wants. And I'm the big bad wolf."

I threw back my head and laughed at Raelynn's garbled metaphor.

"Then what?" I asked. "Ice cream? A guinea pig? Long existential discussion of how life isn't always fair, and you must suck it up, buttercup?"

"Nah," she said. "Hugs and kisses and a dance around the table to 'You Can't Always Get What You Want.'" She stood up and attempted a Mick Jagger move, one so bad I choked on my chamomile tea.

"Hey, sweet pea, it made 'em laugh. Eased the pain.

When their mom picked them up, I figured it was her and my son's turn for the full-scale frontal attack. And how about you? Is that detective still giving you a hard time?"

I wiggled in the recliner, trying my best to look relaxed, hoping my aunt wouldn't freak out over my news.

"More on that later, but here's something wonderful. Do you have room for a temporary guest? I'm flying to Tampa for a visit in a week or so, and if you put me up for a few days, I'll repay the favor by teaching you how to move like Jagger."

Raelynn leaned close to the screen. "Ah, sweetie, what happened? Are you giving up the shop?"

I grimaced. "No. Somebody set fire to the store, and we have to delay the opening until we do some rebuilding. We're looking at early or mid-March now for the grand re-opening."

"Wait! Somebody set fire to your shop? Vic, tell me true now. Are you safe? What's going on?"

I told her. About the death of Dennis. About how the suspects in his death were limited to the people at the private wake for Bernice at Waves End gallery. About how Maccini had discovered my past. And about how I was snooping around.

"Even Maccini can't figure out how the two deaths might be connected," I told her, "and I can't either. Nothing makes sense." I took a sip of my now-cold tea.

"Okay," said Raelynn, who had listened carefully during my recitation. "I'm not going to tell you to stop detecting. You never listen anyway." She smiled to take away the sting of her words. "But I do have a question. Could there be two killers? Maybe someone you don't know killed Bernice. Then maybe one of your Alleton circle killed Dennis for a completely unrelated reason. Sounds like his wife or his son might be suspects."

"I'm having dinner with Tami in about an hour," I told Raelynn. "After she heard about the fire, she called and invited me over. Should I ask if she or D.J. are killers?"

My aunt blew a raspberry at the screen. "You are shortening my life, dear. So promise me, for real, that you won't take unnecessary chances. Two murders are not a laughing matter."

I drew a cross over my heart. "I promise," I said, then switched the conversation to possible dates for my upcoming visit. Raelynn might disagree with me about what "unnecessary chances" means, and I wasn't about to get into that discussion.

31

After that phone call, which didn't resolve any of my fears but did make me feel better, I put on some warmer clothes and headed out to Tami's place.

Her neighborhood was quiet, most of the houses showing the blue light of television screens through front window curtains. The smell of beef stew wafted out as Tami opened her door. Dressed in a dark orange sweatshirt and blue jeans, hair pulled back in a loose ponytail, eyes underscored with black smudges, shoulders slumped, she looked ready for a long nap.

"Come on in," she said, her voice soft. "I'm just finishing the stew, so we can eat right away." She took my jacket, which still smelled of smoke, and wrinkled her nose. "That must have been a shock. All that work, and a damn fire."

She led me to a dining area just off a kitchen that featured dated almond-colored appliances and offered me a chair at an oak table marred by scratches. "I'll get the stew. You want a beer?" A few minutes later I dipped a piece of sourdough bread into a bowl thick with meat, potatoes, and carrots, the hearty dish soothing my battered soul.

"This is just what I needed, thanks Tami. You doing okay?"

She took a swig of beer. "D.J.'s a big help. He's hurting, too, but some of his female friends from school are doing their part to make him feel better." She grinned. "Sometimes

I still can't believe he's my boy. Den and me would look at family pictures and wonder how us two produced what one of his high-school girlfriends called 'a dreamboat.'"

The rest of the meal passed quietly, and Tami and I eased into a comfortable companionship. We both ate a generous portion of what Tami said was her mother's stew recipe, and I eventually stopped, sated. At Tami's suggestion, we moved into the living room. It reminded me of Bernice's front room, the furniture outdated, frayed, and lumpy in the wrong places. Tami perched at the end of a sofa, I sat in a chair, my bottle of beer on the table beside me, and finally broached the subject I was most interested in. "You heard anything from the police yet?"

Tami's reaction ended the easy-going atmosphere. "Do you know that Maccini guy? The detective?" I nodded. "Do you know what he asked me?" I shook my head no. "That big jerk wanted to know where I was the day Bernice died. And where Dennis was, too. Do you freaking believe that? Dennis is dead, and this damn cop wants to know if maybe Den was out killing Bernice a week before he died."

I wanted to know the same thing and was thrilled to find out Maccini had asked, even if Tami was so angry about the question that she could barely spit out the words. "We both were at the shop that day, of course, but he wanted some sort of proof. We had to go to the store, and I had to dig out receipts, some signed by Den, some by me, and do you know how that made me feel, my husband dead and this cop didn't care a bit about that."

She pounded on the arm of the sofa with her right fist, steamrolling through the outrage of that interview.

"After the jerk decided Den and I had not killed the Dragon Lady, he started in on me, and what had I been doing at the wake and did I give Den any poison and you know I've heard you two argued a lot and maybe you thought life would be better without him, and he went on and on like that until I stood up and told him to get the hell out of my sight, and you know what he said, like I should forget he was accusing me of killing Den, he said 'So sorry ma'am, just doing my job, and I know you would want to help me find out who did these murders.' And let's not forget what they pulled with that damn search warrant." Tami, inhaling deeply, finally ran out of steam.

I wanted to ask her about D.J. and his alibi but knew she would shut me down cold, so instead I reached over to take her hand, trying to offer some comfort. The look of fury I got made me yank my hand away and scoot back in my chair, increasing the distance between us.

"And you," she said, "Miss So-Full-of-Sympathy, I gotta think this all started happening once you got to town and talked Bernice into selling the store to you even though her daughter was the one who deserved it and even though Den and I offered a more than fair price 'cause we wanted to move onto the main drag. Maybe that Maccini needs to ask you all those stupid questions 'cause I got plenty of things I'd like you to explain."

Tami's unexpected onslaught was like a slap in my face. Apparently, Maccini wasn't the only one she held a grudge against. But she hadn't asked a question and I was afraid to contradict her perception of my purchase of Bathing Beauty. The last thing she would accept was an argument from me, but I didn't know what to say that would ease her acrimony. Instead, I reached over and picked up the bottle holding a few remaining swallows of beer and cradled it in my hands while willing my heart to beat more slowly.

I threw Tami a quick look, fearful of what I might see, but she was staring off into the distance, her breathing regular, her face calm, her hands relaxed on her lap.

I finished off the beer, set the bottle back on the end table, and cleared my throat. "Ask me what you want," I said, holding my hands out, palms up. "But first I will tell you Maccini talked to me several days ago, same as he talked to Sarah and pretty much the way he talked to you. He's a jerk to everyone."

Tami shifted on the sofa so she could see my face. "I told you once I'm stronger than people give me credit for, and that means I'm not gonna be pushed around." She pointed a finger at me, and her look dared me to disagree. "So you wanna tell me what you offered for Bathing Beauty and what you had over Bernice that she wouldn't sell to people she's known for years?"

"You want another beer?" I asked. "'Cause I could use one." Tami got up, went to the kitchen, and returned with two opened bottles of beer. She put them not-so-gently on the end table, not concerned about water marks. While she was gone, I retrieved my purse from the dining room. I took out my phone and found the information I needed.

"That's my business lawyer's name and phone number. I'll email it to you. And I'll call and give him permission to let you know about the contract." Shades of my angry response to Maccini when he had a similar question went through my mind, but this time I fought hard to keep my voice friendly. "I had nothing on Bernice, and I didn't know about other people in town bidding, and it was strictly business."

If I thought my willingness to be open would mollify Tami, I was wrong. Her next words made the situation even more distressing.

"Sure, I'll call him," she said and pointed her beer bottle at me, "but do ya think he'll explain why you never talk about your dead husband, why you keep your past such a damn secret? I asked D.J. and Kylie, thinking maybe you talked to someone near your own age, and they both said you always changed the subject."

Her look of fury had not abated in the least, and I steeled myself for whatever else she was going to throw at me. It was worse than I expected.

"All this makes me think," she said, her voice almost a hiss, "that maybe your dead husband was an abusive SOB, and maybe you killed Dennis because it's your mission to rid the world of all its nasty men."

32

When I finally got back to the condo, I poured myself a shot of bourbon. It was after midnight, too late to call anyone, so I was left to confront the mess I had made on my own.

My protestations of innocence to Tami did no good, she simply dismissed them with a wave of her hand. And I got no sympathy from Tami when I confessed to her about my past. She listened to my bare-bones recital about Drew's death and the rumors about my involvement and my name change and search for a new life with a stony face, drained her beer, got up and came back with my jacket.

"That's some story," she said, throwing the jacket at me. "Ya got a number I can call to check that one out, too?"

I stood up, put my jacket on, and straightened my shoulders. I didn't think it would help, but I had to make one last try at mitigating the confrontation. "I'm sorry I kept my life such a secret. You didn't deserve my distrust."

"Why," Tami asked, "should I believe anything you say to me when you walked away from your own damn family? I'd say it's been nice knowing you, but obviously I don't know you at all."

* * *

It'd been years since I'd had a hangover, and the idea of trying hair of the dog the next morning made me nauseous. I rinsed the dirty glass that was lying on the carpet near the recliner, where I'd left it after tossing down a couple slugs of bourbon upon my return from Tami's. Drinking was not normally my thing, but the accusations Tami threw at me were an uncomfortable reminder of what I'd faced in Tampa.

My plans for a new life were starting to look like the burned remnants of the Bathing Beauty shop.

I plugged my dead cell phone into the charger, layered a sweatshirt and hoodie over jeans, unable to stand the smell of my jacket, and left the condo, pulling a knit beanie over my aching head. I hadn't bothered to check the outside temperature, 12 degrees or 32 felt the same to me, too damn cold. Outside on the shoreline, the gray skies and cold wind matched my interior misery. I stared down at the sand, hands stuffed in pockets. A dog barked in the distance, and two exercise addicts bid me a cheery hello, but I kept my eyes down and walked and walked, then turned back and walked and walked some more.

Back at the condo, I stripped, showered, and dressed in black jeans, a dark gray T-shirt and a black pullover sweater, then stuck a bagel in the toaster and brewed tea. Sarah and I were meeting with a contractor that afternoon, but the rest of my morning was free. Free to try and make sense out of the enemy I had made of Tami, yes, but also free to see if I could make sense out of the events that Maccini and now Tami wanted to blame on me.

I devoured the bagel and cream cheese, finished my tea, took the dishes to the kitchen, and returned to the table with my laptop. I keyed in the password and looked for the file I had created earlier, which contained the names I'd entered of those who had been at Bernice's wake. I had just started to scroll through the list when someone pounded on my door.

"Lauren, are you there? Lauren, answer the door! It's, it's me, Sarah."

I closed the file and opened one that dealt with Bathing Beauty insurance, then ran to the door.

"Thank goodness," Sarah said as she practically fell into the room, "I've been calling and leaving you messages for ages. Is, is everything all right?" She piled her coat, hat, and gloves on a nearby armchair and followed me into the kitchen. I pointed at the phone on the counter. "Sorry, forgot to charge it last night. What's up? And do you want any coffee or tea?"

"No, we have to go. D.J., he's borrowing a truck so we can move our inventory to a storage facility. We, we need to get to the shop." She paused and took a good look at me. "You look pale. And why are you dressed in mourning?"

I looked down at my black and gray apparel. "Just a fashion statement. Goes with the week. Give me a minute and I'll be ready."

Seeing Bathing Beauty again was depressing. The shop looked so good from the front and so ugly from the back, with black marks marring the rear entrance and bits of ash still floating in the cold air. Unfortunately, after all the work we'd done unpacking inventory, it all had to be moved out before renovation began and drywall dust filled the store. Sarah said she had contacted D.J. and Tiffany the previous afternoon and told them we'd pay for their moving services. They were due in half an hour.

No one except Sarah had left a message on my phone. Which meant Tami had not had a change of heart and called me with an apology. And what about D.J.? Had Tami talked to him? Was I on his bad side now, too?

Sarah and I were in the middle of bringing summer merchandise up the stairs when D.J. and Tiffany arrived.

Strands of pink hair peeked out from under her knit hat, but her cheerful hello was quickly replaced by a sad "Oooh, no," when she saw the burned-out portion of the store. D.J. greeted Sarah and me with coffee and blueberry donuts. I relaxed a bit. Either he had not heard about my transgressions from his mother or had chosen to ignore them. The swirl of possibilities made my head ache.

"Seems like we were just unpacking all this stuff," D.J. said, waving at the shelves. "Easy come, easy go." He went back out and returned with several empty boxes he'd picked up from recycling bins scattered around the back alleys of downtown Alleton. "One of the shop owners came out and screamed at me like I was stealing something of great value from her," he said. "But she calmed down once I told her who needed these. Oh, Cassandra wanted to come by but she's at Waves End today."

D.J. and Tiffany took over moving summer merchandise up from the basement while Sarah and I began the dispiriting task of removing products from the shelves. We also selected those containers too damaged to be sold. "Let's take a picture of these," I said, "and I'll make a list to give to the insurance company. This is a lot of cash going up in smoke."

Tiffany paused on one of her trips. "Maybe what's inside can still be used," she said. "What if I sort through and take some to different charities, like the place that houses abused women? I bet they'd love them." She pointed to a plastic bottle of botanical shower wash, its lid covered with melted soot. "And I wouldn't mind taking that one."

The idea of giving some stuff to charity made the task seem less onerous. Sarah even began humming. Finally, the truck filled, D.J. jumped in and headed off for the storage facility a couple miles from downtown, Sarah and I following in her car. Tiffany offered to deliver the smaller boxes set aside for the charities and said she'd head home after that. Unloading took about an hour. Sarah also decided to go home, but D.J. and I voted to visit the roadside diner for lunch.

I had a lot of questions for D.J. and decided to use the direct approach, just as I had with his mother. My hope was that it would not end as disastrously as it had with Tami.

The usual diner chatter and the smell of bacon offered the comfort I so needed, and after D.J. and I ordered our lunch, a salad with grilled chicken for me, a cheeseburger for him, I dove in. "The police don't seem any closer to solving these tragic events," I said, adding honey to my tea and trying to act nonchalant. "Have you heard anything?"

He looked around the room and leaned in a bit. "Cops aren't telling us anything except 'The investigation is ongoing.' That one detective really upset Mom. She says he practically accused her and Dad of killing Bernice."

I'd heard that from Tami but shook my head in apparent surprise. "That's crazy. Why would he think that?"

"Who knows? Guess they can't solve anything yet and are looking for any suspect they can find. It's terrible."

"Have they given you a hard time yet? Sarah and I have both been through the wringer with that Maccini guy."

"Yeah," he said. "I got the same treatment. And I couldn't come up with an acceptable alibi for the day Bernice died, so I guess I'm still a suspect."

I grinned at him. "Ah, he wasn't buying that you were with one of your many girlfriends?" I asked, hoping to pin him down without it being too obvious.

"You've been talking to Mom," he said, his cheeks turning a light pink. "She's always giving me a hard time about all my 'groupies,' even though I try to tell her most of them are only friends."

The waitress, a teenager who looked cute in the diner's uniform of a red-and-white striped shirt with a red apron over black pants, chose that moment to deliver our lunch. After a few bites, D.J. said, "I'm going back to school in a couple weeks, which means Mom will be by herself. That worries me, but she keeps saying she'll be fine."

I noticed he had not answered my question about where he had been on the day Bernice died but couldn't think of any way to bring it up again. I also couldn't think of an easy way to tell him about my past, to confess to the secret I'd been keeping since before he met me. But I wanted him to hear it from me because Tami would no doubt put the worst spin on it.

The waitress came by, and I ordered more tea. "Hope you're not in a huge hurry," I told D.J. "I need to talk to you about something."

He shrugged his shoulders. "You're not about to confess to murder, are you?" he asked, which drew a startled look from the waitress, who was refilling his coffee.

"No, and that's not even funny." My response seemed to reassure the waitress, who gave me a quick smile and moved on to the next table. "I do confess, however, to keeping some things about my past a secret. Your mom knows about this, and it's time I told you, too."

The waitress returned with my tea, and I waited until she moved away to start detailing my background. D.J. listened closely, not saying a word until I was done.

I took a sip of tea, afraid of what was to come. But he reached over and tapped my hand. "Tell me, which do you prefer? Lauren or Victoria?"

The question broke the spell of tension at the table, but, like his mother, D.J. had more to ask. "I don't understand

155

why you moved away. People can be mean, yeah, but that doesn't seem like a good reason to run."

I struggled to explain, telling him that even my brother and favorite aunt had agreed that a new start might be a good thing.

"You don't know how awful it was," I said. "It seemed like everywhere I went, people were whispering about me. Finding my car vandalized with 'killer' graffiti sent me to a counselor, who spent a year helping pull me out of my grief and anger. The worst was my sister-in-law, my brother's wife, who didn't even want Greg to invite me over for meals when her family was present." The memory of Carmen essentially disinviting me from a July Fourth picnic made me blink away tears.

D.J. patted my hand again. "That's rotten," he said. "But maybe the only way to solve things is to go back and face it all head-on."

If only it were that simple. He had no idea how much I longed for home, even though going back would mean living with constant whispers and sidelong glances, maybe even more nasty graffiti on my car. I sighed.

For now, however, my immediate concern was whether to tell him about his mom's reaction to my confession. Before I could work out the words, D.J.'s phone buzzed.

"Hey Kylie," he said, then listened for a couple minutes, his eyes growing wide. "Is she going to be okay?"

My heart sank. He had to be talking about Evie.

"Okay. I'm with Lauren right now, and we'll drive over. It'll take us about 15 minutes or so to get there. Hang tight."

He disconnected the call. "Evie's in the hospital, but she's doing okay. I told Kylie we'd stop by. She's pretty shaken up."

"I'll get the check," I said. "Meet you at the truck."

As I stood by the table, pulling on my hoodie, our waitress came over and handed me the bill.

"Even if he makes you pay," she said, "I'd keep him. He's a doll."

33

D.J. drove fast, and I expected to hear sirens blaring behind us, a police officer pulling him over for speeding. But it wasn't until we neared the hospital that we were blasted by sirens, as an ambulance whooshed into the emergency entrance.

He parked in the general lot and we rushed to the information desk, where a receptionist told us Evie was in the intensive care unit.

"Are you family?" she asked.

"Yes," I said. "She's my niece. Her other aunt is waiting for us up there." D.J. gave me a surprised look, but fortunately the receptionist didn't see it.

"That was quick thinking," he said approvingly as we walked to the elevator. "I forget about all the rules these places have."

"I'm not going to lie to the ICU nurses," I said, "but it seemed the quickest way to get to the waiting area without the receptionist reciting all the regulations."

Kylie was in the ICU waiting room, and she jumped up when she saw us, sloshing her coffee on her jeans. She made a beeline for D.J. and gave him a big hug. "Oh, thank you for coming. I've been so worried. Christie and Tom are with Evie now, and she's conscious and asking to go home and play, which is a good sign. The docs say she'll pull through, but this really scared me."

"What happened?" I asked when Kylie finally ended her hug with D.J.

"We're not sure. I was on my way back from Chicago and couldn't be here, so Evie was at home, eating lunch with Christie, who took a break from work. Suddenly Evie got dizzy and collapsed. Christie says it was Evie's normal food, so no one is sure what caused the problem. But Evie's system is so fragile that it could be anything. And I'm not sure Christie is as careful as she should be. Evie's never had any problems when she's with me."

D.J. and I got some bad coffee from the vending machine and sat with Kylie, who occasionally jumped up to go around the corner and peek in at Evie.

"You can only have two people in there at once," she said, "and Christie and Tom are staying by Evie's side. I'm just waiting until one of them needs a break, then I can visit with her for a bit."

She sighed. "Still no word on a donor match for her. I put the word out on social media to some Asian-American groups in Michigan, and I'm hoping we'll get someone."

"It'll happen," D.J. said, although to my ears his reassurance held more hope than certainty.

A woman with short dark hair walked into the room. Kylie introduced us, but I already knew she was Christie, Kylie's sister. The two had the same cute pug nose and high cheekbones.

"The best news! Doctors say Evie is on the mend," Christie told Kylie. "Tom's going back to work. I'm grabbing a late lunch, so you and D.J. can go keep her company if you want." She looked at me. "Join me for coffee? I'm excited to finally meet you. Evie talks about you, and it'd be good for us to get to know each other."

Kylie and D.J. headed off to Evie's ICU room, and I

followed Christie to the hospital's coffee shop, which was filled with people chatting in high, nervous voices. Christie ordered a turkey roll-up while I stuck with hot tea. "Thank you for working on the donor match project," she said. "Kylie's friends really came together on that. It means a lot to Tom and me."

"No problem. I just hope a match can be found."

Christie rubbed her eyes. "At least her disease is under control now, but I'm afraid she'll have to start having lots of immunosuppression work until a match comes through. That won't be fun, but she's such a trouper."

We chatted for a bit about the medical options available, then Christie switched subjects. "It was good to see D.J. here. Do you suppose he and Kylie might get back together? She's had a tough time the last few months, lost a big client, missed an investment opportunity, spent hours taking care of Evie." She tore away pieces of her turkey roll-up. "They were a good couple. I think she saw him as the one, but then it all sort of fell apart."

"Any idea why? They don't discuss that with me."

"Not sure. I asked Kylie, but she was kind of vague. I think D.J. might be a bit of a ladies' man, maybe isn't ready to commit to one woman yet. Ah, well, I can't run their lives. I'm just thankful Kylie has the time to watch over Evie. Tom and I would be helpless without her."

Back at the ICU, Kylie and D.J. left Evie's room so I could join Christie and visit her daughter briefly. Evie looked lost in the bed, tubes and wires running from her arms and body to the various machines beeping around her. She held up a hand to me and we exchanged a gentle high-five.

"Mommy, Lauren makes hot chocolate for me!" She giggled. "Can I come see you soon?"

"Chocolate, the way to a girl's heart," Christie said with a laugh. Even though Evie looked wan and tired, at least she was engaged in the moment.

"We had a fire at the store," I told Evie, "so it may be a few weeks before it's ready for a visit from my favorite four-year-old."

"I forgot about your fire, that's such a shame," Christie said. "The stuff going on in this town is unbelievable. I felt so bad for D.J., losing his dad, but he seems to be bouncing back okay. School will keep him busy, keep his mind off things."

Kylie poked her head in. "D.J. says he's ready to go if you are," she told me. I nodded, gave Evie a quick hug, shook hands with Christie, and switched places with Kylie. "Keep me up to date," I said to her as I waved good-bye.

D.J. drove me back to Bathing Beauty so I could get my car, this time following the speed limit.

"Thanks," I said as I stepped from the truck. "That was an unexpected side trip, but I'm glad we could be there for Kylie."

He looked at the blackened back of the shop, grimaced. "Bad luck seems to be following all of us around. Sarah's mom is killed, my dad is killed, your shop is burned, Evie is in the hospital. Makes me wonder what's next on the list."

* * *

Once again, I sat in front of my laptop, staring at the file of suspects I had opened earlier in the day. The gruesome exercise of ferreting out a possible killer called for a glass of wine, but my fading energy level demanded a hit of caffeine.

With the irritating screech of gulls as background noise, I scrolled down the names of those who had attended Bernice's wake, the list I had given to Maccini, and drew a line through those who had proven alibis for the Sunday that Bernice died. Sarah was in Nashville, and Tami and Dennis were at their store. Same went for Natalie. I'd never found an easy way to ask either Kylie or D.J. what they'd been doing that day. And either Frank or Justin, or maybe both, had been working, but I had no proof of which one staffed the gallery that day.

Several people, ones I didn't know well, also stayed on the suspect list but seemed peripheral to the events of the week. Gus the book guy. Tiffany the part-time student and my new employee. Cassandra the part-time employee of Waves End and now Bathing Beauty. The owners of Antonelli's restaurant and the proprietors of several other downtown shops. They were all at Bernice's wake, and they all had to remain as suspects.

Unless I went to each of them and asked directly where they were on that Sunday, I could not cross them off, but their likelihood as suspects was, to me, minuscule. Of course, I thought, hiding in the background might be exactly what a savvy killer would do. Who would suspect friendly Gus or charming Cassandra?

Finally, I highlighted the names of the people who looked like the most likely candidates. The gut-wrenching exercise left me with a short list of people who had become my friends: Frank and Justin and Kylie and D.J. And in case there were two separate killers, a thought I could hardly comprehend, I had to leave Tami and D.J. as suspects in the death of Dennis.

Maccini's remark about means, motive, and opportunity applied to my list, but, like Maccini, I could not come up with a motive for any of them to kill both Bernice and Dennis. Justin probably was addicted to opioids, and D.J. had commented on the fact that Dennis carried a hefty life insurance policy, but neither of those two pieces of evidence, flimsy as they were, got me any closer to a solution.

I couldn't stop asking questions, invading my friends' private lives. The evil had to be stopped before Maccini decided my motive of keeping my identity a secret checked all the boxes, and I was in handcuffs, trying desperately to prove my innocence.

34

"**What is that fabulous smell?**" I asked when Kylie motioned me into her house.

"Making some treats for Evie," she said, "and I'm taking some to the nurses, they do so much, and they deserve recognition, too."

I'd texted Kylie before I went to bed. She was the easy one to start with since we had business to discuss. She replied to my text of "can I drop by for 30 minutes or so tomorrow to discuss social media needs following the Bathing Beauty fire?" almost immediately, telling me to come by any time before 11. Evie was out of ICU and in her own room, and Kylie said she planned to go to the hospital at noon and take her niece a luncheon treat.

Kylie took my hoodie and I followed her into the kitchen, where she peered into the oven. "A couple more minutes, and we can taste-test them. Tea for you?"

She made the drinks and pulled the cookie sheets out of the oven, twirling around in her bib apron that was decorated with dancing elephants, a print Frank would find hilarious. "Grab a place at the table, and we can eat and talk. I already have ideas for you."

"Let's resolve the payment first," I said as I took a seat. "How about I hire you for 20 hours freelance? My brand needs some work, and I don't know what to post on the various sites."

We settled that, and Kylie told me she envisioned playing with the Bathing Beauty artwork, perhaps showing the model splashing waves of water on a fire. "Let me prepare some sketches and come up with a cute phrase. This will be fun."

I picked up a cookie from the plate Kylie had placed on the table and took a bite. Time to jump in.

"You and D.J. shared quite a hug in the hospital," I said. "Have things changed?"

Kylie looked down, brushed some crumbs off her apron. When she looked back up, I saw tears in her eyes.

"I'm not sure I want that anymore," she said. "He worries me."

I raised an eyebrow. "How so?"

"I should keep my mouth shut," she said, "but the jerk doesn't deserve my covering for him. He never even thanked me for trying to save Dennis's life. It's like he wanted his dad dead. Now all he talks about is finishing school."

She stood up, untied her apron, and threw it on a nearby chair. "You just can't trust some people."

I was saved from responding when her phone buzzed, a common occurrence for the social media entrepreneur. Kylie glanced at it. "I need to take this. It's Christie."

She disappeared into her bedroom and I got up and walked around, checking the adorable set-up she had for Evie. Behind the toddler-sized table and chair was open shelving stuffed with coloring books, crayons, various craft projects, a hand-drawn map to a tree fort, a kiddie science set, a jewelry box with lots of butterfly barrettes, Lego sets, and a row of books with colorful covers. All the ways to keep a child occupied without straining her physically.

"Evie's coming home tomorrow," Kylie said when she

danced back into the living room, her earlier anger apparently forgotten, "Christie says the doctors are running a few more tests this afternoon, and unless a major problem shows up, she'll be released." She glanced at her phone. "I should head to the hospital now, but I'll let you know when the sketches are ready. And thanks for hiring me."

"When it's done, I'll share them with Sarah, so she can approve them, too," I said.

Kylie pursed her lips. "Really? I thought you were the one in charge."

"I am, but I like to get Sarah's take on things. She has the background with the shop and I trust her judgment. Plus, I want her to know how much I value her help, maybe eventually make her a partner."

"Makes sense, I guess," Kylie said. "You're a good boss. Now I have to run."

"I'm heading for Waves End. Haven't seen Frank or Justin in ages, and I'm suffering from withdrawal," I said.

Kylie gave me an odd look. "That's one way to put it," she said as she handed me my hoodie.

* * *

Parking was at a premium that Friday noon, a good sign for Alleton merchants. I gave up finding a spot near Waves End but managed to grab a place in front of Bathing Beauty. One of the contractors was due to arrive in a couple hours, so I'd end up back there anyway.

I walked over to Waves End, pulling my hoodie close to stave off the chill. The gallery was open. Once inside, I yanked off my hat and paused as I always did to nod at the angry, androgynous statue in the foyer before entering the showroom.

"Hello," Frank called from his office around the corner. "Welcome, and look around all you want, I'll be out in a

166

minute." A tray of cookies sat on an art deco credenza underneath one of the fabric art pieces I'd seen Justin installing earlier in the week, but I'd eaten my allotment of sugar at Kylie's house.

"It's just me," I called back to Frank, not wanting him to think he had to rush out and charm a real customer.

"Oh, okay," he answered.

My shoulders sagged. Not the cheery greeting I was used to. I walked into the gallery's office, and Frank looked up from his computer.

"Just left Kylie's," I said, adding enthusiasm to my voice, hoping to change the negative vibe. "Evie gets to go home tomorrow."

Frank nodded. "That's good," he said. "And what brings you here?"

I put my hat back on, the chill in the air matched what I'd faced outside. "Still bummed out about the fire and at loose ends waiting to find out when I can open," I said. "Just needed a fix of Frank."

He stood up, scowling at me. "Your choice of words is hilarious," he said. "Any other funny things you want to say?"

I stepped back. "Frank, I don't know what's going on. Why are you upset with me?"

Frank leaned over, signed off his computer, and picked up some papers from the desk. "I can't believe you don't know. Kylie does, seems like she would have told you."

"Told me what?"

"Justin checked himself into rehab. He's dealing with an addiction to pain pills. Which is why your 'fix of Frank' came off as totally insensitive."

Now I understood why Kylie gave me a funny look when I'd mentioned "withdrawal" to her. She must have thought I already knew about Justin.

"I am so sorry, I really didn't know. But that's a good thing, right? Justin getting help."

"Okay, I accept your apology," Frank said, not sounding the least bit mollified. "And going to rehab is a good thing for Justin. What is not so good is all the stunts you've been pulling. You are a piece of work, and not one I would ever want to display here."

I leaned back, unconsciously ducking the spray of vitriol.

But Frank wasn't done. He slammed the papers back onto his desk, stood up even straighter, and narrowed his eyes at me. "Let's start with the easy one. You hire Cassandra, MY employee, and don't even think to talk to me about it. Guess that's what I get for welcoming a stranger into town."

I opened my mouth to tell him that Cassandra asked me not to say anything, and that she was going to stay at Waves End until he found a replacement. I didn't get a chance to state my case. Frank, his face red with anger, brought out the big guns.

"Oh, and I hear from Tami that you came here under a new name. You lied about your background. You act so sweet and innocent, and you act like you care about Sarah being screwed out of owning the shop, and you help with the bone marrow donor program, and ..." he took a deep breath, "and since you got here, we've had two murders and a fire. I can't believe you haven't been arrested yet. For now, you need to get the hell out of my gallery, out of my town, out of my life."

Tami had said the same thing to me, but coming from Frank, it cut even deeper. The guy with the funny aprons, the guy who said he liked everyone, the guy who greeted guests with a hug and a taste of his latest delicacy, the guy who was Alleton's unofficial welcome wagon, had torn away any thought I had that I could start a new life, could leave suspicion and innuendo and outright nastiness behind.

So much for gaining information about the gallery's owners. But if the gloves were off, I could fight, too.

"I haven't been arrested because I didn't do anything," I said, returning his glare. "And if we're going to make unfair accusations, let's talk about Bernice, who was given sleeping meds and sent out into the cold. Who do we know around here who plays around with drugs?"

Frank clenched his fists but didn't move closer. "And Dennis was given a fatal amount of potassium while at a party in your apartment, where you made all the drinks and food."

The recipe in Frank's cookbook for high-potassium Beet Brownies flashed through my mind, but my knowledge of it would have to remain my secret.

"Okay, let's talk about how you could have prepared a special version of your secret orange drink and served that to Dennis. And let's talk about how either you or Justin could have gone to Bernice's and fed her some of your famous cookies, with a little extra ingredient added. You want to talk about that?"

The two of us faced off across the desk. Frank was the first to blink.

"Accuse me all you want, because I know I didn't do it. But I know Justin, and I don't know you. He is the finest man in the world, and I won't have you accusing him."

"I heard some hesitancy there," I said. "Do you know where Justin was the Sunday Bernice died? Did he make cookies that weekend?"

"I said I won't have this," Frank yelled. "You need to go."

I pointed a finger at him. "I had no reason to kill Bernice or Dennis or to set fire to my shop. And I plan to make things right by Sarah. But you're correct, I am new here. And there might be political or business reasons someone in Alleton wanted them gone that I know nothing about." Frank's eyes widened. "Maybe it's time for me to talk to the people who are not in the cozy core group you invited me to and find out what secrets are playing behind the scenes."

We both heard the ding as the gallery's door was opened, perhaps a customer stopping by. I turned to leave the office and could barely hear the parting words Frank muttered.

"Justin is not a murderer, and maybe you are not either. But at least he doesn't pretend to be someone he is not."

His office had no door for me to slam, so my exit lacked any drama. I managed to nod to the two people who had entered the gallery, and I didn't look back as I left.

35

I carried in the chai latte I'd picked up at the coffee shop, left the back door of Bathing Beauty ajar, and pushed open the front door. I found a roll of duct tape in the office and taped a barrier across the doorway to discourage interested passersby from entering the store.

The brisk wind did little to remove the smell of soot and smoke, but the empty space did allow me to sit on one of the office chairs that had survived the fire and relax a bit, get over the shakes of my confrontation with Frank. Apparently, all I was accomplishing was infuriating people.

Sarah wasn't due for another hour. I pulled my phone out of my purse, went to the contacts app, and pressed a name.

It was 2 p.m. on a Friday, and Greg would be at work, probably out overseeing a construction project. I didn't expect an answer and didn't want one. Voicemail, I thought, would give him time to consider his answer, without me hearing the hesitancy in his voice.

When the call went to voicemail, I calmly recited the words I had prepared.

"Egg! It's Vic. Sorry I missed you. I'm planning a trip to Florida. There was a fire at my shop, and the grand opening is delayed for a month, so I have some time on my hands. Call and maybe we can find a date that works for you."

A beep ended my allotted time. I closed my eyes, sending a quick prayer along with the message.

The slender line of duct tape across the open doorway apparently would not keep everybody out. "Hey," I heard D.J call as I stashed my phone back into my purse, "anybody around?"

I got up and walked to the front of the store. D.J. hadn't entered the shop but was standing outside the flimsy barrier. He was sporting a faux fur-lined cap with ear flaps, which made him look like he was about to go trap a bear.

"Come on in," I said, "if you think you can stand the stench."

He ducked under the tape and wrinkled his nose. "Whew, still not good. But I'm not staying. Wanted to tell you Evie is on her way home. Ran into Kylie at the gas station. She is so excited."

"Hey D.J. thanks. I saw Kylie earlier today, and she gave me the news. That's great." I rubbed my hands together to stave off the chill. "By the way, thanks for telling Tiffany good things about me. I'm thrilled she's joining the team."

D.J. ducked his head. "Tweren't nothing," he said.

"Speaking of nothing," I said, putting my tea on a nearby counter and reclaiming my seat, "Kylie told me you two were done, kaput. Sorry about that. Not my business but I thought you two were a sweet team."

D.J. continued to stand. "We might have made a go of it," he said, pounding his fist on one of the counters, the noise making me jump. "I just got tired of her running hot and cold. Playing games. Enough."

I was speechless. I had never seen D.J. angry. And his response to my remark about Kylie had thrown me. What was it with those two? Who could I believe?

"Ah, forget it," he said as he moved toward the taped entry. Before he left, he turned back, motioned around the room's empty shelves.

"You going to stick it out?" he asked. "I wouldn't blame you if you put it back on the market or handed it over to Sarah and went back to sunny skies."

I took a final sip of the chai, the experience made unpleasant by the lingering, noxious odors that permeated the store. "Need some time to think," I said. "And I might make Sarah a partner, if she'll have it, but keep that under your funny hat. For now, I'm the owner of record and have to deal with the renovators and insurance company."

D.J. ducked under the tape, turned, and waved. "You'd make a profit if you decided to sell," he said. "I know a few people who probably still want this place."

Sarah walked up to the front entry, just in time to hear his parting words. D.J. gave her a quick hug and walked away, shoulders slumped, head down. "Are you, do you plan on selling?" she asked, looking across the street where two women were window shopping at the boutique. "Because if you are, you, you should sell to an outsider. Too much inbreeding in this town."

I smiled. "Nope." I checked the time. "We have thirty minutes until that first guy shows up to give us a bid. Let's go to the coffee shop. I need some fresh air."

When we returned, Sarah and I, unwilling to sit in the smelly, cold shop, waited in her car. Somehow, she'd managed to get a space right behind mine. A few minutes later, the renovator tapped on the car window. "Are you the owners?" he asked, pointing at the store. We both nodded. "It's open," Sarah said. "Got it," he said. "I need to go in and take some measurements, look around. Be back out soon."

Sarah kept the car heater running, and we sat quietly for a few minutes, watching some stalwart winter souls making the rounds of nearby open stores. Sarah sighed.

173

"I knew all along Mom wouldn't leave me the store," she said, broaching a subject I'd never had the guts to ask her about. "She, she always wanted me to find my own way. And she was afraid I'd drive the shop to bankruptcy. Kind of, a little funny, right?"

I turned slightly in the passenger seat so I could look at her directly. "Funny?" I asked.

"Oh, she, she was the one who would drive it to bankruptcy. Never wanted to upgrade, make any changes."

Sarah took a sip of coffee, made a face.

"You, you think I don't know people called her the Dragon Lady, but, but I did. Couldn't blame them. She was always so nosy, poking around in everybody's affairs.

"Don't get me wrong. I loved her. But I, I can't help but wonder if her busybody ways are what got her killed."

You and Maccini both, I thought but did not say.

The renovator's knock on the window ended our dark conversation. He glanced at a small notepad in his hand. "I'll get you and your insurance company the bid by next Tuesday," he said. "And I'll do what you wanted and include a separate bid for a spray-tan booth. Fair warning, fixing this won't be cheap."

"Do you have an idea of the time element?" I asked.

"I'm thinking four or five weeks," he said. "Your insurance company will set a deadline with penalties if we don't meet a timetable." He tipped an imaginary hat. "Enjoy your day."

"Penalties sound good," I said after he left.

"Me like, too," Sarah said with a grin. "But, but we need to make sure insurance pays for clean-up. Drywall is the worst."

The second contractor was due in thirty minutes. Sarah turned up the heat in the car and gave me a big smile, her

174

mood apparently lightened by the contractor's mention of the spray-tan booth, her plan approaching reality. "I have some great news to share," she said. "Remember the stakes, those markers in the yard you asked me about?"

I nodded, smiled, hoped I could look surprised at the news she was sharing.

"Well I, I can tell you the secret now! I rented that space, part of a parcel my dad had deeded to me when he died, to a cell tower company. They'll put up a tower in a few weeks and, and my house and the area around it will finally have cell service. I'll get a nice monthly check, too."

"Wow, that is great news. But why was it such a secret?"

"I felt so bad having to lie when, when you asked about it, but the company insisted. They were afraid another tower company might learn their plans, make a deal with one of my neighbors, and, and beat them to the installation."

I glanced away, Sarah's apology filling me with remorse.

When the second contractor showed up, Sarah and I remained in her car while he took his measurements and photos of the shop. He gave us the same timeline as the first guy, said he'd be in touch with details, and took off.

I got out of Sarah's car, went back inside, closed and locked the badly singed back door, did the same to the front door, and exited the shop. Sarah rolled her window down.

"A March opening isn't such a bad thing, because, because a hint of spring will bring out more shoppers, anxious for summer. We'll be okay."

Her determined optimism made me smile.

"Spring?" I said. "Who needs spring when we have such a refreshing, invigorating, cleansing wintry breeze to keep our spirits high?" I shivered, Sarah laughed, and the day suddenly seemed brighter.

36

I made it to the dry cleaners before their 6 p.m. closing. They told me they would have to run my jacket through twice to get out the smell. Not a problem, except that it was 19 degrees out and Florida me didn't have a full complement of winter gear. A couple Alleton shops sold winter coats, but I didn't want anything expensive. Any clothes I wore to the store would be ruined.

Which meant I'd have to take a trip to a big box store in a nearby town. In the meantime, I'd have to settle for being chilly and miserable in a sweatshirt and hoodie.

* * *

Saturday dawned cold and damp, and the frozen shoreline was free of even the die-hard walkers. I settled into the recliner, warmed by a cup of hot tea and serenaded by the raucous calls of gulls and occasional twitter of chickadees.

My tranquility was interrupted by the vibrating phone skittering on the table. The name on the caller ID made my heart jump. Greg, returning my call, the answer to a Saturday morning prayer.

"Egg! Good morning!" I said, my finger crossed.

"You never cease to amaze me, Vic," he said. "Two people are murdered. Your store burns. You need to come home before things get worse."

I wanted to sing with happiness. And I was not about to tell him that I thought my freedom was in danger. That would bring out the implacable older brother, and he would probably drive up to Michigan, throw me in his car, and take me kicking and screaming back to Florida. Which sounded like the better of two possible scenarios.

Still, as much as I longed for my family and the Tampa heat, I was not going to take off. Maccini would probably see that as a guilty person running away, and I didn't need him on my case more than he already was.

"I will come home, at least for a few days. Just tell me what works best in the next couple of weeks for you and Carmen." It hurt to add her name, but this was an attempt to repair a rift.

"Let me check. I'll call you soon with some dates. And, um, did you want to stay with us?"

Bless him, but reality had to intrude sometime. We were not going to be a magical, perfect family for a long time. "Appreciate the offer," I said, knowing one had not been forthcoming, "but I need to stay in the downtown area, meet with my business attorney and some retailers. This will be a part-fun, part-work trip."

"Okay. Let me know if you change your mind. And Sis, I can't wait to see you. It's been too long."

I disconnected the call, tossed the phone on the chair, threw open the slider, and sprang out onto the balcony. I lifted my arms skyward and did a little circle dance. The biting wind drove me back inside, but I came in refreshed, light, free of the weight of guilt and bad decisions.

With no work to be done at Bathing Beauty, I spent part of the day laboring over the shop's financial affairs. Finally, restless with inactivity, I decided retail therapy was called for. I piled on layers and headed to one of the big box department stores in Holland, a quick drive up the interstate from Alleton.

177

The store had already started replacing winter merchandise with spring items, but I was able to find an inexpensive winter jacket I could wear when checking on renovation progress at Bathing Beauty, where the sooty smell of smoke and the drifting drywall would wreck it.

I was more excited by my last-minute impulse buy, an amaryllis gift set with a rustic vase that would fit perfectly with Sarah's country decor. For the next few weeks, she could watch the flower grow as we waited for the store to be ready.

Before anyone else could tell her my idea, I needed to ask Sarah if she wanted to be part-owner of the store. I'd just worked out what I considered to be a decent financial arrangement, and if she agreed, it might end her search for a franchise in Tennessee. That was a plan that I, of course, could never let on that I knew about.

I threw my packages in my car and glanced at my phone, 6:30 p.m., full dark approaching and snow beginning to fall. If I added a stop to relieve my hunger pangs, I could be at her place in an hour.

Sarah answered her landline on the third ring. "I'm in Holland, finishing some shopping," I told her. "Can I stop by your place on my way home? It's okay if you say no, this is really last-minute."

"I could use some company," she said. "All this early evening darkness always gets me down. How about if I, I could make some hot chocolate or coffee, and we could add a little Irish cream."

"A sweet deal! I'll be there in about an hour."

I took my time with my soup and salad dinner at a chain restaurant, again going over the details of what I wanted to present to Sarah. If she had no available cash, she could trade her work hours and small monthly payments for a stake. But if Bernice had left her a nice legacy, Sarah might want to put down a big payment and pay off the rest monthly. I'd have my Florida attorney work up the contract, and she could choose her own attorney to check the details and make sure she was getting a fair deal.

The idea put me in a good mood, even though my continual flipflop of emotions left me a bit on edge. I could not forget about Maccini's suspicions or about the possible danger any of the Alleton merchants were in with a murderous villain still unidentified. But so far, the killer had gone the poison route, and I would be ultra-careful about what I ate at get-togethers from now on. If I was ever invited to another one.

I turned down the waiter's offer of more tea, paid, and headed out the car, where I put on my new black polyester fleece coat, then climbed into the driver's seat. I despaired of ever surviving a northern winter, and my pleas to my car to heat up faster had little effect. A thin layer of snow covered the car's hood, and the flakes were starting to come down harder by the time I was five miles down the highway.

Maybe a stop at Sarah's wasn't such a great idea, but I would pass on the alcohol and not stay too late. And if she agreed to my plan, I knew it would leave me with a warm feeling.

37

Lights showed in the old farmhouse, but the place and its association with death still made me shiver. Sarah now parked inside the garage, since she'd sold Bernice's old Chevy, and a car I didn't recognize was parked in the driveway, so I pulled to the side of it. Whoever Sarah's unexpected visitor might be, they put a crimp in my plan to discuss business.

I picked up the amaryllis, which I could pass off as simply a thinking-of-you gift, and knocked on the side door. A minute later, the door opened, and Eliot peeked out at the new visitor.

"Lauren! Sarah said you were dropping by. Come on in." Kylie, bypassing vintage wear for warm black trousers and a dark pink and maroon cable knit sweater, stepped back, shooing Eliot out of the way. "I came by to share some good news and deliver a coffeepot she had ordered from me, but it seems I'm serving as temporary hostess."

I placed the amaryllis gift set on the kitchen table and dropped my purse and new coat on a chair. Kylie motioned me through to the living room, where I sat on one of the dingy, overstuffed chairs. The low sound of some country music ballad trickled through the radio in the corner.

"This is weird," Kylie said, "because I am so excited about my good news and now Sarah has bad news."

I reached down to pet Eliot and raised my eyebrows at

Kylie. "Let's do bad news first, then good," I said. "Always best to have something to look forward to."

"The bad news is that Sarah's elderly aunt died. She's on the phone upstairs, talking to her cousin. Rose, I think her name is. The death was not unexpected, Sarah told me, but Rose needs help planning the funeral.

"Sad, right? But she'll get through it." Kylie jumped up from her seat. "Let me get us some coffee first, Sarah has a pot ready. Then I'll tell you the good news."

"Oh, two funerals in a short time, poor Sarah," I said, hoping my voice sounded normal, as Kylie walked by me, headed for the kitchen. "But hold up with the good news. I need to hit the bathroom."

Inside the bathroom, which was off the hallway leading to the downstairs bedroom, I stared in the mirror, my mind returning to Bernice's funeral. That's when Sarah had told me that her only remaining living relative was a distant male cousin, one she rarely spoke to. Other memories resurfaced. Gus the book guy talking about a "young hopeful" who wanted to buy Bathing Beauty. Kylie's expensive furniture and clothes, her frequent trips to Chicago, her constant phone calls. Justin's look her way when he talked about being worried that the police might search his and Frank's apartment.

Money to burn, even though Christie told me Kylie's business had taken a hit when she lost a big client.

I didn't have time to think it through carefully, but only one thing made sense. Kylie was a drug dealer.

Had Kylie murdered Bernice and Dennis? What was happening with Sarah? And was I next on the list of people who stood in the way of whatever it was Kylie wanted?

I clutched the edge of the bathroom countertop and took several deep breaths, trying to calm myself. This was no longer an intellectual game of name-the-killer. I had to check on Sarah. And if what seemed an impossible idea was true, if Kylie was a killer, that might mean I would have to disable her.

Advice from the teacher of the self-defense class I took when the rumors about my involvement in Drew's death started to get nasty came back to me. "If you truly are fighting for your life," the instructor, a burly man with close-cropped hair, told the class repeatedly, "you can't hold back. You need to use force, cause some damage."

I reached over and flushed the toilet, ran some water in the sink. "Be strong," I whispered to my reflection.

I exited the bathroom and walked the two steps to the door leading to Sarah's living area. I could hear the clatter of dishware in the kitchen. I opened the door and walked up a couple steps. The upstairs was deathly quiet. I stepped back down, closed the door, and returned to the living room, where I perched on one of the overstuffed chairs.

"You want some booze with this?" Kylie yelled from the kitchen.

"Plain is fine," I called back, "I'm a little worried about the drive home."

When Kylie returned with two mugs, she handed me one with an apologetic smile on her face. "I gave you a bit anyway," she said. "Take a sip, see what you think. And you can follow me back to Alleton. I promise to drive slow."

Steam was rising from the mug, and I clasped it in my cold hands. "A bit won't hurt, I guess. So, tell me the good news."

Kylie, still standing, took a swallow from her mug, set it on a side table and raised her face to me. "Evie has a donor match! Not from Alleton, but one of those Asian-American groups I contacted in the Detroit area. A lot of tests need to be done, but if it works out, the donor agreed to go through the procedure."

I set the mug down on the other side table, jumped up, and gave her a hug. "Kylie, that is fabulous. All your work paid off. I am so happy!"

A tear was rolling down Kylie's face. "Tell me more," I said as I backed away from Kylie. "What happens next? How long will it take?"

"I'm going to think positive thoughts," she said. "And I don't know all the details but I'm talking to the donor match board tomorrow and they'll fill me in."

She reached down and lifted her mug. "Grab your coffee. Let's toast to Evie."

I lifted my mug, clinked it with Kylie's, took a pretend sip. I didn't know if Kylie had drugged my coffee but wasn't about to take chances.

"Why don't you go check on Sarah?" I said. "See if she can join us. She needs to hear some good news, too."

"Great idea," Kylie said, then headed for the upstairs door, carrying her coffee mug. My brilliant idea of switching coffee cups went with her.

Once Kylie disappeared, I hightailed it to the kitchen, dumped my coffee in the sink, and refilled the cup about a third of the way from the pot on the counter. Then I reached over and picked up the landline phone. No dial tone. That was all the evidence I needed. Kylie was lying to me about Sarah.

I was back in the living room, sitting in the lumpy green chair, the coffee cup next to me on the side table, planning what I had to do, when Kylie returned.

"Sarah coming down?" I asked, then took a sip of coffee.

"She's still on the phone," Kylie said. She walked by the chair I was in, and I saw her glance down at my coffee cup.

"She said she'd be another 10 minutes or so. How about I get us some more coffee?"

"I'm good," I said. I pointed at Eliot, who had been rubbing against my ankles. "Did you hear the news, Eliot?" I said, "Evie has a chance to get better!" Eliot performed a little leap into the air.

I stood, picked up my coffee cup, and walked over to the window, lifting the curtains to peer outside. Moonlight revealed snow falling at a steady rate. I stepped back, staggered a bit, then caught my balance.

"You okay?" Kylie asked.

I looked back at her and blinked. "I'm not sure," I said. "I'm feeling dizzy."

Kylie gazed at me, and I thought I saw a small smile cross her lips. "You don't look so good," she said. "Maybe you should ride with me back to Alleton. We can come back and get your car tomorrow."

I nodded, breathing in short gasps. "Can you tell Sarah?"

"No problem," Kylie said. She turned and moved back to the stairway. I dumped the rest of my coffee in a nearby potted plant and remained standing by the window while a guy on the radio sang about a broken heart. "Sarah sends her apologies, said she'll call you tomorrow," Kylie said when she returned. She walked to the sofa. "You want to stretch out on here for a minute? You really don't look well."

I took a couple wobbly steps toward her, blinking my eyes rapidly. When Kylie reached out a hand to steady me, I tightened my grip on the handle of the heavy ironstone mug and hit her in the face with it. I heard the satisfying sound of her nose breaking. Kylie fell sideways onto the sofa, and I grabbed her right arm and twisted it hard behind her back. Kylie let out a muffled scream and started kicking her legs and twisting her body, trying to dislodge me. I twisted her arm up higher, and Kylie screamed louder.

I jumped off the sofa, ran to the kitchen, and yanked my cell phone from my purse, my eyes trained on the kitchen doorway. I punched in 911. Nothing. Of course. I'd forgotten about the sketchy service in Sarah's neighborhood.

I heard movement in the living room, dropped my cell phone on the kitchen table, and backed up fast as Kylie, blood streaming down her face, her right arm held close to her body, stumbled into the kitchen.

Kylie staggered forward, and I saw a glint of something in her left hand. Her eyes narrowed, and she moved in close. I grabbed the back of a kitchen chair with my left hand, and the glint caught the kitchen light and slashed through my left forearm. I managed to lift the chair and swing it toward her, walloping her right side. She let out a screech, stumbled, and fell to the floor.

I stepped closer, looking for the glint I'd seen in her hand but didn't see it, then jumped over her body and ran for the stairs. In the hallway at the top of the stairs, I opened the door on the right, fearful of what I would find.

The room was empty. I opened the other upstairs doors onto rooms also empty. I ran down the stairs, slowing down as I neared the bottom, checking for signs of Kylie. She was not in the living room. I edged around to the kitchen. No Kylie, but the outside door was open.

I knew it could be a trick, she could be hiding inside, but I needed to find Sarah. I picked up the kitchen chair that was lying on the floor and turned to my left. Holding the chair in front of me, I took small steps toward Bernice's bedroom, my eyes darting back and forth.

The bedroom door was closed. I stood to the side, chair in one hand, and reached over, turned the knob and pushed the door open.

I peeked in the room and saw Sarah lying crookedly on the bed. I pushed the door harder, so it slammed against the wall, making sure Kylie wasn't behind it. I walked backward to the bed, my eyes on the closet door, set the chair down and reached over to touch Sarah. She was breathing evenly, and I shook her gently. "Sarah, wake up. Sarah, it's Lauren. You have to wake up." In the distance, I heard a car door slam and an engine starting.

Huddled on my knees, I put my right arm under Sarah's shoulders, carefully cradling her head, and saw red drops falling from my left arm onto the white tufted bedspread. I kept calling Sarah's name. In what seemed like a lifetime, she finally wiggled a bit and moaned.

"Sarah, please, you have to wake up. Now. We have to go."

Sarah turned and looked at me. "Lauren? Is that you?"

I hugged her tightly and pulled her body to a sitting position.

"What, what, why are you here? What happened?"

"You're hurt," I told her. "We need to drive to a neighbor's house and call for help."

It took several minutes for me to maneuver Sarah to her feet. She laughed when I put my right arm around her waist and nudged her forward.

My left arm was throbbing, and blood was still seeping through my hoodie. I saw nothing amusing about the situation, but Sarah took a different view.

"Whoopsie!" she said. "Am I drunk?"

I was finally able to get Sarah to the kitchen, where I leaned her against the table, draped my new jacket over her, and grabbed my purse. Several awkward moves later, I got her out the door and into my car. The other car was gone.

Eliot bumped against my leg, and I scooped him up and put him back in the house, closing the door on his plaintive pleas.

Full dark had arrived, and an icy wind whistled through the trees. When I got in the car, Sarah appeared to be asleep. I jostled her, and she shook her head and grinned at me.

"Whatever Kylie gave you," I told her, "looks like fun."

A half mile down the road, I pulled into her closest neighbor's driveway, laying on the horn to get someone's attention. When an older gentleman eventually hobbled out the door, waving his hands, I stopped honking and rolled down my window.

He walked over to the car, glanced at me, then peered past me at Sarah, who was snoozing gently in the passenger seat. "Sarah, is that you? What's wrong?"

"Help me," I said. He started to walk around my car, and I jumped out and joined him outside on the passenger side. I opened the door, joggled Sarah, who lifted her head and moaned. Her neighbor and I managed to get her out of the car and into the house, where we guided her to a sofa.

It took much longer than I wanted it to, but I convinced the gentleman to call an ambulance because Sarah had been drugged. I told him to call the police, too.

"I have to go," I said. "The woman who did this took off. I need to find her. She's a murderer, and I'm afraid she's going to hurt someone else."

I stepped outside.

"But you're bleeding," he called to me from the front door as I got back in the car.

"Get help for Sarah. I'll let the police know what I'm doing as soon as I'm in cell phone range."

I gunned the engine and took off into the swirl of snow. A few miles down the road, I decided I might finally be able to get phone service. I could call the police from the car and continue my trip toward Alleton. Just before I reached in my purse, I pictured that moment at Sarah's when Kylie staggered into the kitchen and I'd dropped the phone. It was still on Sarah's kitchen table. I saw the lights of the roadside diner ahead on my right. Should I stop there?

My car slid on the icy road, and I clutched the wheel harder, wincing at the pain where Kiley had sliced my left arm. Kylie had already killed two people. I had no idea what she planned to do next, but I feared the worst and wasn't about to let her escape. I passed the diner and hunched forward in the seat, peering at the side of the road as I pressed hard on the gas pedal, fighting to stay on the slippery pavement.

38

About a quarter mile from Christie and Tom's house, I pulled my car into the woods, hiding it behind a small stand of trees. A sliver of moon turned the night ghostly. I walked toward the mansion, not getting too close, until I could see from peering behind a tree that its windows were dark.

I made my way to Kylie's cottage, which also was dark, and in the pale moonlight I found a well-worn path leading through the woods. I followed it until I stood several yards from the giant oak in whose lower branches Kylie had built a tree fort. It was Evie's "secret place," the one I had seen on the map I had found on the shelves by her toddler table at Kylie's.

I heard what sounded like singing and moved a bit closer, still staying out of sight. The low crooning and rushing wind covered the sound of my advance. The cover of trees began to thin, and I dropped down and crawled to a thicket of bushes.

Cold seeped through the knees of my jeans as I raised my upper body and peeked through the bushes. I stifled a gasp of dismay when I saw Kylie, blood smeared on her face, sitting on the ground under the oak tree, a blanket-wrapped Evie cradled in her left arm. I knew Kylie could reach Evie's bedroom from a side door but hadn't thought she would risk taking her niece out into the cold. I was wrong.

Knowing I might also be wrong about what I was going

to try, I still had to take a chance. Evie might be in danger from the cold, but she could be in even more danger from her aunt, a stone-cold killer.

I picked up a small, thick stick and lobbed it over the bushes. It landed to Kylie's right. She started and looked around the clearing, although the darkness kept her from seeing me.

"I know someone's out there," she called. "Is it you, Lauren? Go ahead, show yourself. I can't hurt you."

She might still have the knife, but I didn't think she would let go of Evie to come after me. I stood up, parted the bushes, and walked into the clearing, careful to stay out of her reach.

"You're quite the fighter," she said, pulling Evie closer to her body. "Another one of your secrets?"

"No," I said, sitting on the frozen ground several feet from her. "I took a self-defense class after Drew died." I hesitated, then held out my arms, blood dribbling down my left hand. "Do you want me to hold Evie? I could take her back to your cottage, get her warmed up."

Kylie let out a strangled cry. "You're like everyone else," she said. "Always taking things away, never giving me what I want."

"No. I just want to give Evie some hot chocolate. You could come with me." The cold was seeping through my flimsy hoodie and jeans, and I was feeling faint. I had to get Evie and myself inside before I passed out.

"Do you know what Bernice said to me when I asked if she would sell me her shop?" I shook my head, but Kylie wasn't paying attention to me, she was staring off into the distance. "She laughed, said she wasn't about to sell to a drug dealer."

I was right about the explanation for Kylie's deep

pockets, her ability to buy expensive clothes and furniture.

"When I went to her house that Sunday, I asked if she would teach me what I would need to know. I told her I was done selling drugs, I knew it was wrong. And I could run the store and not have to run around so much looking for web clients."

"She still said no," I guessed. "And you made nice, handed her one of your poisoned cookies, and you ate one of the safe ones."

"We each had two. The Dragon Lady even made me tea. But when I left, that cat somehow got out the back door, maybe because I threw a cookie out onto the yard. I convinced Bernice we had to find him." Kylie laughed, an eerie sound, and Evie stirred in her arms. I wondered if Kylie had given her something to help her sleep. "Bye-bye Bernice."

I scooted closer, getting a better look at Kylie's face but still unable to see if she had a weapon somewhere. Kylie turned and looked directly at me.

"Don't get too close," she said, and I shivered at the malevolent sound of her voice. "You don't know what I'll do."

"Okay," I said. "Just checking on Evie."

"You think I would hurt her? I love her. I was the one who paid for that bloodmobile. You don't think I'm good enough? Be careful. That's what ugly Dennis thought, too."

"What about Dennis?" I asked. If I could keep her talking, immersed in her own anger and memories, I might be able to get even closer. "What did he take away from you?"

It was hard to tell in the dark, but I thought she was crying. "D.J.," she said, "he took D.J. My soulmate, the one I could build a future with, the one who would help me raise

Evie once I took care of my always-busy sister and her money-hungry husband."

I couldn't stifle my gasp. For the first time, I realized that trying to talk sensibly to Kylie had little chance of success. But Kylie was back in her own world and didn't react to my exhalation of horror.

"Dennis saw me when I was outside the toy store a few times, supposedly waiting for D.J., but noticed that sometimes I'd hand a small package to a person walking by. That stupid jerk figured out I was dealing and said if I didn't break up with D.J., he'd tell my sister, and she would never let me take care of Evie again."

While Kylie talked, I dug my heels into the cold ground and dragged my body forward, moving closer by inches. I trembled with cold or fright, it was hard to tell which. The left arm of my hoodie was soaked with blood.

Kylie hugged Evie even closer. "I thought D.J. would be thankful that I tried to save his dad's life. It was so cool when Dennis died. Then I could be with D.J."

She turned and looked at me, chin up, eyes narrowed. "You," she said, spitting out the word. "You acted like my friend, and then you introduced D.J. to that Tiffany and …" she slowly shook her head. "I was hoping you'd be tired of this place and leave once I burned your shop down. But no. You wouldn't go away. That's when I decided to burn you and Sarah up in her house. I would have laughed and laughed. And then I could buy Bathing Beauty."

She suddenly seemed to realize I was sitting right beside her.

"Kylie," I said, reaching out my right hand to touch her shoulder, "you're shaking. You don't have any more body heat to share with Evie. Let's go to your place, get warmed up."

I was shaking too, and so dizzy I wasn't sure I could stand up even if Kylie let me take Evie. She looked down at Evie and then looked away.

"They'll take me to jail. No one understands me. No one knows what I would do to keep her safe. They'll just take me away."

Kylie's eyes widened, as the reality of her words hit her.

"It's over for me, isn't it?" she said.

Before I could answer, she pulled Evie close and kissed her cheek, leaving behind a smear of blood. Evie, eyes closed, sighed softly. Kylie put her right arm under Evie's legs, grunting at the pain the movement cost her, then held her out to me. I reached out and accepted the gift.

Kylie stood up, her left hand holding her right arm close to her body. She looked down at me.

"You'll take good care of her, won't you?" she asked.

"You know I will," I said. "But you need to call an ambulance. Please, you need to keep Evie safe."

Kylie sniffled and pointed at Evie. "Tell her I love her. I always will."

She turned and walked away, not toward her cottage but farther into the woods.

I opened my hoodie and tucked Evie inside. I held her tiny body close to mine as I rolled onto on my right side, protecting her from the wind as the world turned dark.

39

The mid-March grand re-opening of Bathing Beauty was not an unqualified success. It was still too early in the season for a rush of customers to show up. But we did okay, and my new business partner, Sarah, was pleased. She was already booking slots for the new tanning booth.

After the close of business that day, several Alleton merchants stopped by to join Sarah and me. We each raised a glass of champagne and feasted on appetizers supplied by Frank, who gifted me with a "Never be afraid to take a whisk" apron. Justin gave me a quick hug and whispered that he had just earned a recovery button from Narcotics Anonymous. Even Tami showed up. We were still not best pals, but thanks to D.J. speaking on my behalf, the door had a crack in it.

The big surprise was the appearance of Detective Maccini, doing his friendly community cop bit. I was happy to see him. When I came to in the hospital after the horrendous events, he had been my first visitor.

"What happened?" I asked him. "You said Evie is okay? Is that true? How long have I been here?"

Maccini pressed a button, raising the level of the bed. "Yes, Evie really is okay. She's already home and doing great. The doctors think she was given some cold medicine to make her sleepy, but at least she stayed warm. And you've been here about 10 hours, stitched up, warmed up, rehydrated. Docs say you are doing fine,"

The details of that sad, frightful evening with Kylie had slowly come back to me. "And Sarah? How's Sarah?"

"Good. Doctors pumped her stomach, no fun, but she came through with no ill effects."

There was one person he hadn't mentioned. "And what about …" I couldn't say her name.

"We got a 911 call, that's how we found you and Evie in the woods."

I recalled my last minutes with Kylie. She must have made the emergency call.

"Where is she?"

He looked down. "Some cross-country skiers found her body curled up next to a tree in the state park. The coroner thinks she took some drugs and just started walking until she couldn't walk anymore. Huh."

A nurse entered the room and checked the level in a bag hanging by the bed. "We're just hydrating you. An aide will bring you some food in a little bit." She turned and left, her shoes squeaking on the tile floor.

Maccini said he needed to hear from me what had happened while it was still fresh in my mind. For the next several minutes, I related the tragic events as he ran a recorder.

"Need to talk more later, but for now, you have visitors waiting to see you. And Lauren," he hesitated, then gave me a rueful smile, "I had two murders to solve, and nobody gets a pass on my watch when it comes to finding the perpetrator. I was keeping an eye on Kylie, too. We were pretty sure she was dealing."

I took a deep breath. "Part of that was my fault," I said. "I shouldn't have kept my past a secret. I'm sorry."

The counselor was back. "Huh. Apology accepted. But

from now on, Victoria Lauren," he added, "call the police when bad things happen."

40

A couple weeks before Bathing Beauty's grand re-opening, I flew to Florida. My visit to Tampa included a barbecue at Raelynn and Garrett's house. It was 78 degrees, a late winter heat wave for Tampa, and I felt like a butterfly in my shorts, flowered sleeveless top, and slingback sandals, released from my Michigan-winter chrysalis of a dark coat and sturdy snow boots.

Self-proclaimed "King of the Grill" Garrett cooked ribs, burgers, and chicken; Mom and Dad shared stories of their volunteer work in Haiti, but only after my mom, always Wanda the Worrier, finished lecturing me on the chances I took when I went after Kylie; and Aunt Raelynn, Greg, Carmen, and I applauded Roberto's attempts to do a cartwheel.

"I have an announcement," I said when the meal ended, wiping away the sauce on my hands and getting up to stand at the head of the picnic table.

Everyone stopped talking, and Raelynn shot me a concerned look.

"Relax," I said. "I think you'll like it."

Before I left Alleton for my Florida visit, Sarah and I had a long talk. "I want to give up working at the shop," I told her. "I'll stay here through September, then I'm moving back home." She was already co-owner of the store, buying in with money she had inherited from her mother, and didn't need me to make a success of the business she loved.

"Oh, oh, Lauren, I, oh, I will miss you. But, but it's a good thing, you should, you need, I think …" she gave up on the verbal calisthenics and threw her arms around me. "You need to go home," she said. "And, and you can find a new business there."

"So," I finished my announcement after sharing the details of my plan with my family, "I'm coming home."

Aunt Raelynn, I saw, was crying, and Garrett gave her a big hug. Mom and Dad applauded.

"Just in time, Vic," Greg said as he walked over to stand by me, putting his arm around my waist, "Because you'll be around to welcome Roberto's new sibling. Carmen's due in late September."

I looked over at my sister-in-law, who beamed at me.

It was a beginning.

* * *

Early on the day my flight would take me back to Michigan, I went to the cemetery and knelt by Drew's grave. The words of the scrawled message he left for me on that fateful day were seared in my brain.

"Never reveal what I did. It would destroy Carmen. Promise me. I love you. Be stronger than me."

I didn't find the note I had tucked in the pocket of my cargo shorts until several hours after Drew died. Sitting alone in our bedroom, overwhelmed by grief, I learned that he could no longer live with the demons of what had happened in Iraq, a nightmare he refused to share. He had leaped willingly to his own death.

And keeping his secret, protecting his vulnerable sister, became my own nightmare.

So many times, I had wondered if I should have shown

the note to Raul when he accused me of murder. And all those times, I knew I could not trust him with the secret that was not mine to share.

Leaning forward, I traced the engraving of Drew's name on the tombstone. "I forgive you," I whispered. "Rest well, darling Drew."

I stood up, took a long look at the gravesite, then walked out of the cemetery, lifting my face to the warmth of the rising sun.

Acknowledgments

If you've gotten this far, that probably means you read the book. And I owe you a big thank you for giving my novel a chance. If you enjoyed *All the Deadly Secrets*, please leave a review on Amazon. That would mean a lot to me.

My early readers were priceless and deserve more than the free lunch I gave them. Heartfelt thanks to my patient husband, Jim Wensits, who listened to me talk about the book for months before I would let him read it; my fabulous sister, Barb Lane; and my dear friends, Gayle Dantzler and Linda Diltz, whose keen sensibilities and sharp eyes helped me make this a better work.

And special thanks to the extraordinary Kerry Prugh, who designed the cover.

About the author

Carol Schaal, who is always surprised and pleased when the perennials she planted in her yard bloom in the spring, lives in northern Indiana with her husband and their cute dog. As managing editor of the award-winning *Notre Dame Magazine*, she edited articles by such writers as Tom Coyne, Brian Doyle, Paul Farmer, M.D., Heather King, Jamie Reidy, Arienne Thompson, comic Owen Smith, and poets Beth Ann Fennelly and Samuel Hazo. She recently left the magazine world to focus on fiction and discovered the joy of making stuff up.

Made in the USA
Middletown, DE
31 October 2019